The Cursebreaker

The Cursebreaker

Yuna Farah

VANTAGE PRESS
New York

This is a work of fiction. Any similarity between the names and characters in this book and any real persons, living or dead, is purely coincidental.

Cover design by Susan Thomas

FIRST EDITION

All rights reserved, including the right of reproduction in whole or in part in any form.

Copyright © 2008 by Yuna Farah

Published by Vantage Press, Inc.
419 Park Ave. South, New York, NY 10016

Manufactured in the United States of America
ISBN: 978-0-533-15910-9

Library of Congress Catalog Card No.: 2007906819

0 9 8 7 6 5 4 3 2 1

To my mother, my father, and my two brothers, Joseph and Albert. Also, to my four friends: Dillon H., Shelby M., Catia R., and Nadya V.

Acknowledgments

When I first started writing this book, it began as a dare. I thought, *I couldn't finish this, even if I tried!* I remember that day well. It was the Saturday of Thanksgiving weekend, the year of 2006. It was about two months into my last year of middle school. I attempted to write a couple of books quite a few times; I never finished even one. What made me think I would finish this one? Well, I did. And I would like to thank some people for helping me:

I would like to thank my father, who dared me to write this book; my mother, who encouraged me and who gave me the time to write; my two younger brothers, Joseph and Albert, who also gave me the time to write and left me alone to work on my book when I asked them to. I would also like to thank my four friends: Dillon H., Shelby M., Catia R., and Nadya V.; you really inspired me and kept me going through the eight months I had been working. Thank you so much!

I also want to thank Vantage Press, Inc. for doing a terrific job on publishing *The Cursebreaker*.

I want to thank the people who have helped—and offered to help—me with this book, as well. Last, but not least, I would like to thank all my readers who (hopefully!) enjoyed this book. It means a lot to me. Thanks everyone!

Glossary

Damaé—Life and Death
Katé fàre chaté—Open, let me in
Feu—Fire
Feu resvel—Fire arise
Feu proppello—Shield me from fire
Feu naversoi—Fire vanish
Naversoi—Vanish

1

As the sun set in the distant horizon, sixteen-year-old Cedric peeked out from behind his living room curtains.

The colors of the sunset reflected in his wide, blue eyes. Cedric had chestnut-colored hair, which was always tousled. He was part elf and part human, which was not unusual where he lived.

The tall, lanky boy had lived alone for eleven years inside an old brown house on a cliff on the edge of the Trilife Forest. It had a huge, rotting oak door with a heavy bronze-plated knob. The knocker was also made of bronze, but instead of being simply u-shaped, it was a fine carving of a lion's head with its mouth open. There were about three windows on the one-story building. There was a bathroom, one bedroom, a living room, and a kitchen. Cedric ate in the kitchen, which was a decent replacement for a dining area.

The house was an inheritance from his dead parents. The death of his parents was a mystery to Cedric. Nobody told him what happened, and the problem was he never knew *how* to find out the facts of this tragedy. This all changed, however, as Cedric stepped outside the large oak door.

2

The frost-coated grass crunched under Cedric's feet. Bow and arrows slung over his shoulder, Cedric looked out into the distance. Sorrow filled him when he saw the land below marred from previous disasters and wars. The sky, though, made his heart lighter as a result of the silhouettes of flying birds against the different colored sky. He wondered, *How could the sky stay so beautiful while its brother, the land, is constantly being scarred by war?* With this question in mind, he entered the Trilife Forest.

* * *

The Trilife Forest is a wood surrounded by myths of its name of origin. One of the most popular myths is also about the magical creatures in the forest. Each unique being who lives in the forest is said to have been blessed with three lives, hence the name Trilife Forest. The animals in the forest are supposed to be magical, with uncanny powers. Since none of these mystical creatures have been seen before, many people consider them to be made up. However, there is a great majority who believe in these fabulous beings.

* * *

As Cedric walked through the dense, green, dark forest, he wondered what he would encounter. He heard the many tales told of the place and memorized the map of the forest, but yet, he never stepped foot where most dare not go: the heart of the Trilife Forest. The center of the woodland area has a clear blue lake called the cursed lake of Alya.

Alya was a beautiful, clever enchantress who set a

curse upon the waters after being sentenced to drown in the lake, accused of treason to the king of Tora. Her last words were later translated accurately to, "Curse this wretched lake in which I perish! May the Cursebreaker come after the land of Tora has suffered greatly!" Ever since those meaningful words, Tora suffered a great many nightmares. Wars, diseases, and horrors one does not wish to experience have plagued this once peaceful land. The citizens of Tora have waited patiently for the Cursebreaker. It is said that they are losing hope. Their hope is the only thing that prevents the downfall of Tora. If the hope of the people becomes extinct, even greater disasters are expected to befall the city.

There are also other rumors which state that one may learn his or her past and who they are if they visit the Cursed Lake of Alya. There is a terrible price, though. A prophet spoke it:

When one comes to the Cursed Lake of Alya
The sacrifice is receiving a curse
With the exception of the Cursebreaker.

Finding out who he was was the only reason for visiting the accursed lake, despite the heavy price.

Mulling over the story of Alya, he suddenly found himself on the shores of the lake. The sparkling blue water mesmerized him.

"It's beautiful," he breathed.

He stood there for a minute or so, until the sudden hooting of an owl brought him to his senses. Getting down on both knees, Cedric cupped the cold water in his hands and held it up to his face, wondering if he should do this. He shook his head, as if wanting to rid his mind of the thought of turning back and completed the ritual. Simultaneously, as the water hit his face, there was an explosion behind him. The unexpected movement caused Cedric to be knocked down, head first, into the lake. Standing up, dripping wet with water from head to toe, he spun around and with one arrow fit into his bow, and faced his surprise: a unicorn.

3

Cedric and the unicorn stood for a moment, each pair of eyes fixed on the other's face. Cedric cautiously lowered his armed bow, took a step forward toward the unicorn, laid his bow and all his arrows before the creature, and kneeled on one knee.

"Rise, stranger," the creature said.

Cedric stood and gazed at the unicorn with a mixture of awe and respect. She was snow white with sad, sparkling cerulean eyes. A silver, twisted horn protruded from her forehead. About fifteen hands high, her eyes were level with Cedric's blue ones. She had a muscular body; her shoulders were rounded and she stood upright. Her face was relaxed, but Cedric could see that all her muscles were tense as if ready to run or fight back in any case of danger.

"My name is Serena," she said, her clear, bell-like voice ringing with authority and tranquility. "And yours is . . . ?"

"Cedric," the boy replied.

"Cedric," the unicorn said thoughtfully, "you must be here for a special purpose, I assume."

"Yes, I-I am."

"Very well. Come with me."

And both Cedric and Serena began to walk eastward, the setting sun casting long shadows on the ground. Little did they know that they were stealthily being followed.

4

"So," Serena said, "tell me about your purpose for summoning me."

As the two continued to walk, Cedric poured out the whole story, about how he wanted to find out how his parents died and who he really was. He ended the story with the question, "That is my purpose. Is it okay if I ask you something?"

"You just did," Serena snorted, looking at Cedric with amusement dancing in her eyes.

"Seriously."

"Yes, you might as well."

"Well, what did you mean, I 'summoned' you?"

Serena sighed. "I am the keeper of the lake."

"Keeper?" Cedric asked sounding confused.

"Yes. When someone comes to the lake and performs the ritual, I am summoned."

"Oh."

The two walked in silence through the forest. Cedric broke the silence by asking, "Where are we going?"

Serena replied, "We are going to the edge of the forest where I am going to give you directions on how to get to Belle."

"Belle?" Cedric looked questioningly at the unicorn. "Where is that?"

"*She* is the *person* who has the answers to all your questions, not me."

"Why n—"

"Quiet!" Serena suddenly ordered. "Listen," she said more softly.

Cedric listened. That's when he heard it—the crunching of twigs and leaves. Then, from the bushes to his left, darted a brown-colored horse with a slim, hooded rider. Having put an arrow in his bow in record time, he shouted, "Halt!"

Miraculously, the horse stopped. "Go!" cried the rider. "Go you damned horse! Move!" No matter how hard the rider tried, the horse would not budge.

Cedric and Serena ran to the horse and rider.

"Get down," Serena said in a stern voice that Cedric had not yet heard.

The rider reluctantly dismounted. Cedric grabbed the reins to assure himself that the rider would not jump on the horse and gallop away.

"Take your hood off and show us who you are," the unicorn commanded.

With hesitation, the rider pulled the hood back with a black-gloved hand. Cedric gasped. The rider was a girl.

5

She was the most beautiful girl Cedric ever saw. She, too, had chestnut hair, just like Cedric, though it stopped at her shoulders. However, unlike Cedric, she had brown, almond-shaped eyes and freckles. Her lips were pursed, as though she was worrying about something; her eyes were smoldering as though hating herself for being caught, especially by a unicorn. She stood erect, as if saying, "I can handle anything you throw at me."

She was wearing tight, black pants and a tight, black shirt. On her shoulders rested an ankle-length, black cloak, its hem woven with gold thread. A sword, with a deep purple stone embedded in the hilt, hung from the girl's belt. She wore heavy-looking black boots that had four silver buckles on each.

Her eyes met Cedric's, but she quickly focused her stare on the unicorn. They lingered on the face of the magical creature before glaring at her horse.

"Your name," Serena said suddenly.

"What?" the girl said in surprise.

"I said 'your name.' What is your name?"

"Teagen," the girl mumbled.

"How old are you?"

"Fourteen."

"Are you traveling alone?"

"Yes."

"Why were you eavesdropping?"

"Er—because I saw him," Teagen muttered, nodding in Cedric's direction, "and I thought I might see what he was doing."

"And . . . ?" Serena prompted.

"And I followed him."

"And . . . ?"

"And I saw the explosion."

"And . . . ?"

"And I heard the conversation. Satisfied?" Teagen asked testily.

"Yes, I am," Serena said, sounding tad bit amused at this girl's impatience.

"Where'd you get this h-horse?" Cedric asked unexpectedly, his voice quavering slightly.

Both Teagen and Serena turned to face Cedric. They were both surprised to see the boy pale.

"Why?" Teagen asked in surprise.

"P-please. Tell me," the boy pleaded.

"I found him," said Teagen.

"W-where?"

"In this forest. Why are you asking?"

"Do you want to know why the horse did not listen to you when you told him to halt?" Cedric asked, ignoring Teagen's question.

"You should *never* answer a question with a question," the girl chided. "But I have to admit, I *do* want to know."

"Yes, do tell us," Serena muttered resignedly.

"Because he used to be mine!" came the unexpected answer.

6

"Yours!" Teagen and Serena chorused.

"Yeah, mine . . ." Cedric breathed. He surveyed the horse from all angles. "Yeah, Watch."

Cedric walked over to a tree about a hundred yards away and called to the horse. "Tico, come here, boy!"

The horse obeyed. Trotting over to the boy, ears perked up. Tico held his head up high. Teagen and Serena watched in amazement as the horse laid his neck on Cedric's shoulder, nickering softly.

"I have never seen a horse behave like that," Serena murmured.

"Neither have I," Teagen said admiringly.

Cedric walked back to the two. "So," he said to Teagen, his blue eyes dancing with happiness, "what do I have to do to get my horse back?"

"Nothing," Teagen replied. "I'll buy myself a new one."

"Thanks." Turning to Serena, he asked, "What about this friend of yours—Belle, I think is her name?"

"Ah, yes. Belle," Serena said, closing her eyes. "Ride to Sunset Valley. Cross the Anka river. Walk south until you see many cliffs. If you look closely, there are several words in the Forgotten Language etched into the cliff," she paused, making sure that Cedric knew what the Forgotten Language was. He didn't. She explained that it was a language formed thousands of years ago, which is now forgotten by most living in the present times. After the explanation, she resumed her instructions. "Say them, and you should be allowed to enter."

"Allowed?" Cedric asked, fidgeting.

"Yes. Allowed. Belle stays hidden from unwanted eyes."

"Oh."

"What about me?" asked Teagen innocently.

"You shall accompany Cedric," Serena said simply.

The two teenagers answered at the same time. "She will?" Cedric asked.

"I will?" Teagen cried.

"Yes," Serena answered. "However, you may need another horse and supplies."

"We can get everything at Rotera. It's nearby," Teagen offered. "Plus, I've got some money."

"Good. Now, get on the horse and ride. I hope to see you soon."

"Bye, Serena. Thanks," Cedric said sadly at the prospect of saying good-bye to this majestic creature.

"Good-bye, Cedric. I dare say we'll meet again soon enough. Now off you go."

Cedric leaped up on the back of the horse, grabbed the reins, and helped Teagen up. The girl held on to his waist as they rode off into the night.

As Serena watched them disappear around a corner, she reared on her hind legs and cried joyously into the night, "The Cursebreaker has come!" Then, carefully lowering herself down, she galloped back into the deep, dark, silent forest.

Yet, the sage unicorn should have remembered even the wise ones can commit foolish acts. She should have remembered that yelling in the Trilife Forest at this time of night could alert dangerous beings and bring serious consequences. She definitely did not realize that someone heard everything that was just spoken, and it was not Teagen. And this would bring grim results.

7

A black-clothed figure emerged from behind the bushes.

Making sure that the unicorn left, he began to follow the two riders. *Hmm,* he thought. *The Cursebreaker has come, eh?*

Stealthy as a cougar and quiet as the breeze, he made sure that the boy and girl did not leave his sight. When he sat down to rest, it was dawn. *I must report to my master soon,* he thought.

Climbing to the top of a pine tree, he gave an unearthly, bone-chilling screech. There was a *whoosh* and the man climbed down the tree with great agility to meet a face shaped from fallen leaves in the middle of the air. It was the evil, notorious, mangled face of King Hsetah, ruler—or more like tyrant-of the empire Lîtherïä.

"So," his cold voice reverberated throughout the forest, "you finally reported to me. For a while, there, I thought you went off and decided to live with the ducks in the nearby pond. Just look at your shameful appearance," the king added disdainfully, "covered in muck and leaves."

"I am sorry, my liege," the man muttered stiffly, bowing, his voice making the sound of a rattle. "I have recently heard that the Cursebreaker has been found."

"*Whom* have you heard from, Tal?" King Hsetah said sharply to the man, alert.

"The unicorn, the Keeper of the Lake, announced it, my liege, thinking she was alone."

"But she was not."

"Correct, my liege. I have been following the so-called Cursebreaker on foot for a while now. Apparently, he has no idea what—or who, for that matter—he is."

The king let out a hiss of satisfaction. "Good work. We must find the Cursebreaker and destroy him, before he finds out his purpose. Follow me, Tal."

The face in the dead leaves vanished with another *whoosh*. Tal looked momentarily at the ground, staring at what were the brown and red leaves, just realizing that they had turned black and frosty. He followed his master, disappearing in a ring of fire, which burned anything it touched except the being that called it.

8

After galloping for some time, Tico decided he wanted to trot. Surprised at the sudden change of the horse's pace, Cedric exclaimed, "Hey! Why—?"

Tico stopped, turned his head around to face his rider, and snorted.

"I think he's saying that he wants to take a break from galloping," Teagen explained in a sleepy tone.

Amazingly, Tico nodded his head, as if understanding what the exhausted girl had said. Cedric laughed. "Well, then! Trot you may!" And Tico happily began trotting again.

After a time, Teagen's head drooped. When it touched Cedric's back, her neck immediately snapped up again. "I'm *so* sorry," she murmured, a little bit flustered.

"That's alright," Cedric said. "I'm sure you're tired. I don't mind."

"Thanks," Teagen mumbled.

Teagen eventually fell into a tranquil slumber, with her head resting on Cedric's shoulder. Cedric smiled thoughtfully as Tico kept a steady pace.

9

It was around noon when Teagen was waken up by someone gently shaking her shoulder. "Wake up, Teagen. Wake up," said a quiet voice.

"Lemme 'leep," the girl mumbled and rolled over.

"Teagen, wake up! We have to go to that place of yours so we can get some supplies," the voice exclaimed.

"Fine, fine." Teagen rolled over again and opened her eyes. Two urgent blue ones gazed at her. She sat up. "Mornin'," Teagen grumbled.

"Good afternoon to you, too," Cedric returned, grinning widely.

A bowl of berries and fruit were nearby. "Eat these," Cedric said. "We'll ride to the city after you finish and get a decent meal."

As Teagen ate, Cedric whittled a stick. When she finished, she stood up and announced (rocking back and forth on her two feet). "I gotta go."

"Go behind the bushes over there," Cedric muttered, still whittling.

"What?" Teagen half shouted in surprise. "Go behind the bushes? Are you crazy? That is *so* unsanitary. I—"

"Well, then," Cedric said, looking up from his wooden creation, "looks like you're going to have to wait until we get to town."

Teagen grumbled, "No fair. Why don't they put a toilet in these forests? Aaaa!" She walked into a rosebush while pacing back and forth and talking to herself.

Teagen resumed her pacing after plucking the thorns out and rubbing her sore legs, and kept at it until Cedric finished. While Teagen was trying to invent a way of lugging a toilet around the forest, she heard a sweet, low musical note behind her that sounded as pure as glass. She turned around and saw Cedric playing a pipe, which he made out of the small stick he had found. He played a lively tune as Teagen smiled. *Wow,* she thought, *he sure knows his music.*

When Cedric finished, Teagen praised him. "You play well," she said.

"Thank you. This," Cedric said, holding the little instrument out to her, "is for you."

Surprised, Teagen accepted the gift and murmured her appreciation. "Wow," she whispered, studying the artistic grooves up and down the piece of wood. "It's amazing. You did a terrific job."

"Thanks. Now, shall we go to town?"

The girl nodded her reply. After putting the pipe in her pack, she and Cedric climbed on Tico and galloped away.

10

Meanwhile, trouble was brewing in the private hall of King Hsetah's castle. There was a line of seven creatures, which greatly resembled men, wearing black pants and sweaters with hoods that were constantly being worn, not to mention a black mask pulled over each distorted face. Each of them had a belt around their waists that contained a variety of weapons and some provisions.

"Now," the king hissed, "I want each of you to track the mortal I've been telling you about. Split up and search in different places. Once you capture the human, bring him to me. Alive." His red eyes gazed at the seven black figures before him. He himself was clothed in black; a cloak over a tunic with a hood pulled over his hideous face. "I want the boy soon. Before he achieves much. Before he even finds out who he is. If he does, this will mean war."

The seven figures nodded. They understood what this meant. They *must* be successful.

"Your horses," the king continued, "have arrived." He clapped his bony, claw-like, stark white hands. The main door opened, and in came a servant with seven tall, black, fierce horses. The seven beings mounted their horses and looked at their master expectantly. King Hsetah put his fingers together, elbows propped up on the arms of his throne. "You may go," he growled, "but may the heavens above help you if you fail!" The seven nodded, turned, and left the private hall to complete their mission.

The king lowered his hood after his servants left, looking in a broken mirror. He saw a reflection of who he was, inside and out: he didn't like it. He knew he was evil down to the very bone. Even the mirror showed it. The mirror showed his cold, red eyes; rotten, yellow and black teeth; a heavily scarred face, stretched over gaunt cheekbones; and a hawk-shaped nose that had been evidently broken many times. His bald head was tattooed with skulls that seemed so real, as well as evil descriptions pointed all over the side of his head and down his neck. The king lifted the mirror off the wall and smashed it on the floor. After putting his hood back on, he quietly left the room.

11

Cedric and Teagen galloped into the gates of Rotera.

"My friend, Lara, lives here," Teagen explained to the guards at the gate. "We won't be here long," she added innocently, her eyes wide.

The guard nodded and motioned for them to go inside. Cedric let out a gasp once inside the city. "This is truly an extravagant city," he murmured.

"I know," Teagen said cheerfully. "Let's go."

They mingled with the townspeople for a while. There were many different kinds of shops around every corner: candy shops, tool shops, food shops, hair salons, bars, restaurants, cafés, and so much more. Cedric was particularly fascinated with the golden-domed building in the center of Rotera, which was, as Teagen said, the governor's home. The city was fantastic.

They soon stopped at a stable filled with horses. The two dismounted and the stable boy took Tico and walked into the building adjoining the stable. "Lara?" Teagen called.

"Teagen? Is that you?" a voice with a slight accent called from the stairs above them.

"Yup."

Feet pounded down the stairs and a girl came running into view, and she hugged Teagen. She was slender, about the age of nineteen, with short, sandy-blonde hair and soft, brown eyes. "It's so good to see you again!" she exclaimed delightfully.

Cedric, meanwhile, coyly stood in a corner, trying not to interfere with this reunion. Teagen, however, took him by the hand and introduced him to Lara. "Lara," she said, "this is Cedric. Cedric, Lara."

"Well, hello," Lara asked, surveying him with her steady gaze "How d'you do?"

"Very well," Cedric replied. "And you?"

"Good. Very good. 'Specially delighted at seeing my old friend again."

"Same here," Teagen said. "Lara, we need to talk."

"Alright. Follow me." Lara led them to a small, neat, windowless office. "Sit down," she gestured at two chairs politely. "So, tell me. What's happened?"

Then and there, Teagen related the whole story to her friend, starting with seeing the unicorn's appearance, hearing the conversation—not forgetting the bit about Belle—and ending with the need of supplies.

"Very well," Lara said. "I'll help you."

Teagen gazed attentively at her friend. "Any news?" she said suddenly.

Lara looked at Teagen in surprise. "About what? Oh. Yeah. They're still looking."

"Wait a minute," Cedric said hesitantly. "*What* are you talking—?" He closed his mouth almost immediately after receiving a glare form Teagen.

"Well," Lara said after an awkward silence, "I'm sure you want to rest, so you may have the room on the third floor, second on your right."

"Thanks," Teagen said, getting up.

"No, problem."

"C'mon," Teagen said to Cedric. She took the key from Lara, and the two ran up three flights of stairs. They found their room and opened the door.

12

As Teagen and Cedric entered the room, they were greeted with a beautiful sight. The red-orange sun, backed against a pink and light blue sky, was setting over the rolling, green hills. Slowly, they could see house lights being turned on, one at a time. The two stood transfixed, gazing in awe at the scene unfolding before them.

"Well, then," Cedric said, yawning, "we really should get to bed." He walked over to one of the two comfortable beds in the room and dropped himself on it, falling fast asleep.

"Well, *then*," Teagen muttered to herself, "I think *I'm* going to go and take a nice hot shower. After I've used the toilet."

Teagen went into the bathroom and locked the door behind her. She took a long, hot bath—after using the toilet, of course. When she finished, she went over to the other bed and went to sleep, wondering what tomorrow would bring.

13

Both Teagen and Cedric woke to the sound of someone pounding on their door.

"I'll get it," Teagen offered.

She strode across the room and opened the door. Lara rushed in, holding a long thin package.

"Teagen," she cried breathlessly, "you won't believe it! This package came in a few hours after you two came up here. The wretched postman woke me up while I was having a nice rest. But that doesn't matter. I had to open it—please forgive me for doing so, it's for security reasons—and look what I found!"

Lara handed the rewrapped parcel to Teagen. Teagen turned it over and glanced at the label to see whom the addressee was.

"It's for Cedric," she announced, handing it to the surprised boy.

"For me?" he asked, staring at the box in his hands. "Who'd send me a package? Who would send me *anything?*"

"Oh, stop gawking at the *box* and see what's *inside* it!" Lara said impatiently.

"Alright, alright," Cedric murmured.

He opened it. He grasped what felt like a handle and pulled. To his utter amazement, out came a sword. In its golden hilt were three large stones: a square diamond, a round emerald, and a square sapphire. Although the weapon had a silver blade, gold hilt, and three gems—all of which were genuine—it was surprisingly light. As he swung the sword, the blade glinted in the sunlight that poured through the blinds. When the boy first held the sword, he felt as though it was specially made for him and only him. However, little did he know that this special sword was stolen from his most dangerous enemy, whom he was bound to hear from soon.

14

King Hsetah was in a state of fury. "Who would *dare* steal my sword, the great Sword of Damaé?" he roared. "When I get ahold of that thief, I shall tear him to shreds! How dare that fool steal the weapon that took me years to get ahold of! It's the only damned weapon that could kill that fool, the Cursebreaker! And me! Aargh!" He pounded his fist on the armrest of his black, ivory chair; it cracked.

"Tanto," he shouted to his advisor, "get a wizard immediately to repair this chair. After that, see to it that no one disturbs me."

With that said, the king vanished in a cloud of smoke. With a command to obey, Tanto set himself to his task. Within the hour, a wizard expertly fixed the armrest.

When the king returned, he settled himself into the chair and, putting the tips of his long, bony fingers together, he bowed his head and devoted himself to thinking about the theft of his precious sword.

King Hsetah was the only being alive in the gloomy room, with the exception of the occasional cockroach that would scuttle across the black and white marble floor. But those tiny creatures wouldn't count because, once he saw them, the king would lazily lift a finger, a jet of bright white light coming from it, and the poor bug would explode into pieces. King Hsetah cackled whenever he did this, but would eventually slide into his long, quiet moments of brooding about the Sword of Damaé again . . . and again . . . and again.

15

"Well, I really do think we should get our supplies," declared Teagen. "Thank you very much for your hospitality, Lara. We really appreciated it." Cedric nodded his head in agreement.

"Going so soon, are you?" Lara asked disappointedly. "Well, it was nice to see you again. I *am* going to miss you both very much."

And so, Teagen, Cedric, and Tico wandered throughout the city. They bought enough supplies to last a very long time. The last stop was at a stable filed with horses waiting to be sold. Teagen searched for a horse that was suitable for her. She finally decided upon a chestnut mare that had a blaze and four stockings. The horse was descended from the cavalry horses of Rotera; evidently proud of her family history, the mare held her head high. The owner of the stable declared that horse to be ". . . clever, yet stubborn, proud, yet headstrong, and gentle, yet fierce . . ."

Teagen fell in love with the horse almost immediately and wanted to just lead her out of the stable at that very moment, but had to haggle with the owner for a decent price. Teagen came out of the stable with a triumphant look on her face. Cedric surveyed his companion's choice. "Fit for a queen," he stated. "What're you going to name her?"

"Umm . . ." Teagen said thoughtfully. "I think I'm going to name her . . . Zenubia."

"Excellent choice. Let's get going, now, before it gets dark," Cedric said, even though the sun was still high in the sky.

The two then mounted their horses and rode out of Rotera's city gates.

* * *

The two had ridden many miles before they stopped to rest. They stopped near an isolated lake among green grass, which was thriving under the warm sun. While the horses drank from the lake, Teagen and Cedric had some lunch. When they finished, the two laid down and talked as they watched their horses playfully nip each other.

"Tell me," Cedric said, after describing his daily life. "Where do you come from?"

"Me?" Teagen said distractedly. "Well, I come from a place called Catéadreâl. It's a beautiful city, it is."

"What's your family like?"

Silence.

Cedric turned to face Teagen. He was stunned to find tears streaming down her face.

"Teagen, what's wrong?" Cedric asked gently, sitting up.

Teagen sat up, too. She began to sob. "I'm sorry I'm so s-sorry," she cried.

Cedric wrapped his arms around the girl's quivering shoulders. Teagen just collapsed into his arms and began to cry even harder. "Shh," Cedric said. "Cry all you want. I'll stay right here until you tell me what's wrong."

Teagen wiped her eyes on her sleeves. "I'm sorry," she whispered. "I just miss my parents, that's all. I ran away from home a few months ago."

"If you miss them so much, why don't you go back?" Cedric asked.

"You wouldn't understand."

"Try me."

"Well, I'll start with who I am. I am the princess, and the only heiress of Catéadreâl."

16

Cedric gazed at the girl in astonishment. Here he was, holding a runaway princess in his arms. He then realized that there were clues to her identity that presented themselves to him, but he had dismissed them; the way she carried herself, the beauty, the coolness, the cleverness, the choice of her *horse*, for land's sake . . . Why didn't he see it sooner? He pondered this as Teagen continued.

"I found out that I was to be wedded to Prince Jonah of Latel."

Cedric looked up sharply.

"Yeah, I know. He's such an imp. I hate him."

"How'd you find out?"

"Eavesdropped."

"Not surprised. I should've known."

Teagen grinned sheepishly through her tears. "Well, as I was saying, I found out. Then, I ran away from home. I traveled by foot to the Trilife Forest where I found Tico. You know the rest."

Cedric stared into space. He felt jealous of the prince for his plans to marry the girl. For some odd reason, Cedric felt he had to protect Teagen. He then realized how much he loved her.

He rested his chin onto Teagen's head; she was still cradled in his arms. "Are you happy with your decision?" Cedric inquired.

"Course I am. No way I was going to let myself be married to that—that *pig*," Teagen retorted as she stood up.

Cedric yawned. "Gosh, am I tired! I think I'm going to take a nap." He stretched and lay back down again.

"I'm sorry," Teagen said coyly.

" 'Tis alright. I don't mind at all." Cedric then closed his eyes and fell fast asleep.

17

Cedric woke up about an hour later. He looked to his left and saw Teagen peacefully sleeping beside him. He gave her a loving glance. *When should I tell her?* he thought. *Not now. It's too soon.*

He stood up and whistled to Tico. The horse came obediently to his master with Zenubia following. Cedric made sure the straps from the saddle were tight and secure. He patted Tico on the rump and the horse trotted away with the mare still following him. Cedric absentmindedly put his hands on his hips. As he did so, he felt the ice-cold hilt of his new sword. He unsheathed it and inspected it once more. Engraved under the emerald gem were the words "Sword of Damaé." He gazed at the words, lost in thought, when a hand was placed on his shoulder. He spun around and saw that it was Teagen.

"Give some warning, will you? Don't do that again!" he exclaimed.

"Alright, alright. No need to lose your head," Teagen said, exasperatedly, and handing Cedric his bow and arrows.

"Thanks," he said. "Almost forgot those."

"A wise fighter should never forget his old weapons while enchanted with a new one," Teagen said sagely.

"No need to lecture," Cedric said, grinning. "We're not in a classroom."

"One needn't learn in a classroom." Teagen spread her arms out wide, indicating the area. "A calm place like this would be perfect."

"Whatever you say," Cedric said. "But we need to get moving. The sun is going to set soon and the last thing we should do is sleep out in the open."

"Fine. Let's go."

The two called their horses and mounted. They raced most of the time, and by the time the sun set they reached a mountainous area full of caves.

"Which one?" Cedric whispered.

"Er . . . that one," Teagen said, pointing to a medium-sized cave to their right.

They ventured in. The cave was large enough for the riders and their horses, with plenty of room left to spare. It was dark, eerie, and chilly. The horses huddled together for warmth. Teagen murmured a few words and a small fire began to burn.

"You're a-a *wizard!*" Cedric said, surprised.

"Witch," Teagen corrected. "I'm a witch."

"Wow."

"I know."

"That's—"

"Well, well, well. What do we have here?" said a voice from behind them.

Cedric and Teagen froze. They hadn't realized that there were two others in the depths of the cave, hidden by the darkness. The question was, were they friends . . . or foes?

18

Cedric turned around. To his incredulity, he saw a boy about his own age, with a girl standing behind him, eyes wide. The boy had sandy-blond, crew cut hair and deep, crystal-clear, gray-blue-green eyes. He was tall and athletic looking. The girl had mahogany, shoulder-length, straight hair and sparkling brown eyes. She was also tall and slim. They were both dressed in black. Cedric and Teagen heard soft nickers behind the two strangers. Out of the depths of the cave appeared two black horses.

"Well, who're you?" the boy demanded.

Teagen slowly stood up. "The same question is asked here," she said.

"Who are you?" the boy asked again, ignoring Teagen.

Cedric's mouth dropped, but no sound came out. After a few seconds, he asked, "Theo? Is that you?"

"Cedric?" the boy's voice cracked.

"Theo, you remembered!"

The two boys hugged each other as if they were brothers. There were tears of joy and happiness running down both faces. The girls looked at each other uncertainly. "Are we girls missing something?" Teagen asked hesitantly.

"Oh, Teagen," Cedric said. "This is my best friend, Theo. We haven't seen each other in years." Then, turning to Theo, he said, "And who is this lovely girl behind you?"

Theo introduced the girl to the other two. "This is my fiancée, Lorelei."

"Fiancée? You're engaged?" Cedric asked incredulously.

Theo nodded happily. "Ran away together. Parents didn't approve of the marriage. I have no idea why, though. She's perfect."

The girl blushed. "Hello," she said shyly.

Cedric and Teagen nodded a greeting.

"So, Cedric," Theo said. "Who's this behind you? Your girlfriend?"

Cedric turned red. "Uh, n-no," he stammered. "This is Teagen."

"Hello," Teagen muttered.

Theo and Lorelei returned the greeting. Lorelei put her hand on Theo's shoulder. "Please join us for supper," she said.

Cedric and Teagen accepted. The food was delicious. Afterwards, Teagen arose from the small picnic-in-a-cave meal and announced, "If anyone doesn't object, I think I'll go outside."

"Be careful," Cedric warned.

"I will."

Teagen left the stuffiness of the cave and breathed in a gulp of fresh air. It felt good. She sat on a ledge and looked up at the stars. "I wonder if I'll ever fall in love like Theo and Lorelei," she wondered aloud.

"Maybe someday you will," came Cedric's voice from behind her. Cedric sat on the ledge beside the pretty girl.

"When will that day come?" she sighed.

"I don't know. I don't have the answer for everything, you know," Cedric chuckled.

Teagen sighed again. "Still . . ."

The princess yawned. Her head drooped onto Cedric's shoulder. She soon fell asleep. After a while of stargazing, Cedric picked Teagen up, brought her into the cave, and placed her on a cot that Lorelei had prepared for her.

19

Teagen awoke the next morning, staring blankly at the rocky ceiling; she could not remember where she was. Then, all of the events of the day before came back to her in a rush. She rolled over and, not knowing that she was in the cot, found herself face down on the floor. The next thing she knew, someone's feet were on her back.

"Whoops," yawned Cedric. "Sorry 'bout that. Didn't see you there. Lemme help you up."

He stooped down and helped the girl to her feet. She swayed unsteadily, and Cedric had to support her for a few minutes.

"Thanks," she mumbled, still shocked from her fall.

"Shall we have breakfast?" Cedric asked.

"Breakfast? Oh, yes, breakfast," murmured Teagen, a bit confused. She shook her head as if to get rid of some cobwebs in her brain. "Oooh," she moaned. "I've got such a headache!"

"Are you all right?" Cedric asked with concern.

"Yes, I'm fine. But what a fall!"

"Well, let's go to breakfast right now. See if you'll feel better after."

Teagen agreed. She was hungry, and it felt like an eon since she last ate. She and Cedric advanced into the "kitchen." They both ate with Theo and Lorelei. When they were done, Cedric stood up and said, "Thank you very much for your kindness. But we really should get moving now. We also wish you the best of luck on your marriage."

Teagen nodded, also standing up. "Thank you" was all she could muster.

"You're very welcome," Lorelei said. "We really hope to see you soon."

The four went outside, and Cedric and Teagen got on their horses. They said good-bye and rode away. Theo sadly watched them go, whispering as if to himself, "Good-bye, old friend. Good-bye."

20

The riders rode slowly in silence. Teagen was still thinking about how much her head hurt. Cedric, on the other hand, was thinking about his conversation with Theo after he made sure Teagen was asleep. He confided in his friend, telling him how much he loved Teagen and how much he desperately wanted to tell her.

"You should wait a while," Theo had said.

"But how long is 'a while'?" Cedric had asked.

"You will know. Just let your fate unfold," his friend replied.

Cedric brooded over this conversation until he realized that Teagen wasn't with him. He spun Tico around. He searched frantically for Zenubia's hoof beats, but they were nowhere to be found. What could have happened to them?

21

Teagen was furious with herself. She reprimanded herself silently for being such a fool. She not only endangered her life, but Zenubia's, as well. At the moment, she sat upon the poor horse's back, flanked on each side by royal soldiers.

Well, she thought, *they found me. I must escape*!

She straightened her posture, lining up her back up against the thin pole that was fitted into her saddle. Her hands were bound behind her and around the long stick. One of the royal soldiers, sensing her movement, turned his head to face her. "No way you're 'scapin' us, missy," he said, giving her a toothy grin. "Those knots were tied by the best," he continued, nodding to a fellow soldier.

Teagen gritted her teeth. No matter how hard she tried, she couldn't undo the knots. She slumped back against the pole, exhausted. She knew that she did not have a chance, anyway, even if she did escape. Teagen was an excellent fighter, but she knew she could not defeat ten of her father's best men; they were too well trained. She closed her eyes and remembered what her fighting instructor, Gano, once told her: "If you are ever captured and unable to escape, just wait it out. Help will eventually come."

Teagen sighed. *Oh, Gano,* she thought, *I'll wait it out. The question is, will help come?*

22

Cedric eventually found a number of hoof marks near a bush. His brow creased with worry. There were signs of a scuffle followed by a set of organized tracks that led from the scene. Since it seemed that his best bet was to follow the prints, he urged Tico on, leading himself to an expected—yet unexpected—encounter with Catéadreâl's top royal soldiers.

* * *

It was dusk when Cedric came upon a camp with several soldiers sitting around a campfire. The boys frowned. He tied Tico to a tree with a bit of rope and hid behind a clump of bushes.

The soldiers had already set up two tents, one of

which was larger than the other. A soldier came from the smaller tent. "The *princess* is all set for bed," he chuckled.

Cedric's eyes narrowed. He gripped his sword's hilt but then relaxed his hold. *No need to fight,* he told himself.

Cedric crept to the back of the tent that Teagen was in. He listened, making sure no one else was inside. He then sliced a large portion of the tent with his sword and stepped inside. He nearly roared with rage at what he found. There, in the middle of the tent, was Teagen. Her hands and feet were bound with rope and attached to a pole that supported the tent. Cedric strode over to the girl, whose head was bowed, and quickly cut the bonds with his sword.

Teagen looked up in surprise. She cried out with relief. "Oh Cedric," she said, "I'm sorry for—"

Cedric placed his hand over her mouth and listened. He heard footsteps approaching. "Let's go!" he hissed.

He grabbed Teagen by the wrist and walked through the opening he made in the tent. They had gone only a few yards before they heard a shout amongst the men; "She got away!"

Cedric and Teagen broke into a run. It was difficult; there were trees left and right and roots that were uprooted that were barely a foot apart. It was not long before the soldiers reached them. By then, though, the two had reached Tico. Cedric and Teagen leaped on Tico's back, and Cedric cut the knot on the tree with one swift motion.

When the soldiers saw Cedric and the princess together, they stopped in their tracks. Never had they seen such unity between two beings before. In the eyes of the soldiers, Teagen and Cedric seemed one. However, their instinctive immobilization did not last long. The leader let out a great cry and the group dashed forward and attacked the two teenagers and their horse.

Cedric slew the men upon Tico with great ease, as if he had fought in a battle many times before and this was nothing compared to the major fights. When he stopped and absentmindedly gazed at all the corpses with blood gushing out of the fatal wounds, Teagen gently touched his shoulder and whispered, "We've forgotten Zenubia."

Tico trotted back to the soldier's camp. Teagen got off the horse and retrieved hers, which was tied up with dead men's horses. She not only freed Zenubia, but the others as well. Then, mounting Zenubia, she rode back to Cedric. Without a word, she and the boy rode under a waxing crescent moon that hung alone in a starless sky.

23

Cedric and Teagen rode side by side in utter silence.

When they finally settled down and had a snack beside a blazing fire, Cedric encouraged Teagen to tell the tale of her capture. She was reluctant at first, but then, realizing that Cedric rescued her, she decided he had every right to know.

"What happened was this," Teagen began, "I had gotten a little bored with looking straight ahead at nothing but dirt for hours. I decided to look around and explore our surroundings and catch up with you later. I saw a large, bright green emerald sticking out from a clump of bushes. I thought we could take it and sell it for money we could use in case we ran out of supplies. So I guided Zenubia to the bushes, got off, and picked it up. The next thing I knew, the soldiers captured me. It was a trap," she added sheepishly.

"Did you know the soldiers?" Cedric asked quietly.

"All I know is that they worked for my father," Teagen said. "He sent them out to capture me and bring me home. Remember when I asked Lara if there was any 'news', and I tried to avoid further conversation on the topic when you asked?"

Cedric nodded.

"Well, I was asking about the soldiers. I didn't want you to know. I was afraid you'd abandon me."

Cedric rubbed his forehead thoughtfully. "So," he said. "The summary of your *fantastic* story is that you go to a bunch of bushes and get yourself captured?"

"*Fantastic?* I don't know about fan—" Teagen said heatedly, but she was cut off.

"Do you *know* what you did?" Cedric asked, his voice rising in anger. "It was so unlikely that I would have found you. You didn't even make a *sound* about where you were going!"

"Just listen for a—"

"No. *You* listen," Cedric stood up, now yelling. "I have ten men's blood resting upon my shoulders. Have you any idea how it feels to be a murderer? Yes, I know I did it in self-defense, but those soldiers were doing their *job*. I could've rode on without you, but no. I didn't. You know what? If you ever do something like that again, I'm going to keep on going and never look back!"

When Cedric finished his tirade, which continued for another fifteen minutes, Teagen's brown eyes were wide and brimming with tears. "I'm so sorry, Cedric," she whispered. "I really am. Please, *please,* forgive me. Please."

Cedric's enraged face softened. He sat down next to Teagen and said gently, "Of course I forgive you," he said, taking her hands in his. "I'm sorry for yelling at you. I must have sounded like a madman."

Teagen smiled weakly, tears silently crawling down her face.

"I-I was just worried," he continued. "That's all."

"I'm glad to know you care, and I'm *really* sorry," Teagen mumbled.

"That's okay." Cedric sighed and lay back, closing his eyes. "Just *please* promise me you won't do that again."

Teagen gazed at Cedric's handsome features that were painted with light and shadows from the fire before replying, "I promise."

24

While Cedric and Teagen were many miles away from Rotera, something strange was going on in the city itself. Black-clothed riders on black horses were scouting Rotera for a certain sixteen-year-old boy. Lara found this out after awakening to the pounding on her inn's main door in the wee hours of the morning. She tumbled out of bed and sleepily walked to the door; she was still in her plaid pajamas. She opened the door to find a thin male, who towered over her, with a scrawny horse. He was dressed in black from head to toe and wore a black mask with three holes in it: one for the mouth and two for his yellow-green eyes. His hood was pulled low over his masked face. "Yes?" Lara said uncertainly, wide awake by now.

"Let me in," the man growled. "I have traveled very

far." His horse snorted and nipped at his rider's elbow. "*We* have traveled far," he grunted.

"Er, would you like a room?" Lara asked, stifling a giggle.

"I didn't come here for a *room,*" he sneered. "I came for information."

"Well, come in," Lara said, disliking her visitor more and more by the minute. However, knowing that she had to play host for any type of visitor, she led him into her newly furnished lobby, wondering what he wanted to know. She gestured politely to an armchair and then sat in one herself. "What do you want to know?" she inquired.

The man eagerly leaned forward in his chair and lowered his voice, "I need to know if you have seen a boy."

Lara let out as snort of laughter. "A boy? A *boy?* Are you *serious?* Ha! Which one? I've seen so many boys, with running the inn an' all."

"Well," the man said, letting the word roll off his tongue, his upper lip curling. "I'm looking for a boy who is said to be the Cursebreaker."

Lara gasped. "Nah ah," she whispered. "The Cursebreaker? He has come?"

"Yes," came the reply, "and I need to find him." Lara didn't think it was to invite him to a party.

The man then launched into a detailed description of the boy, watching Lara's face closely.

Lara realized who the boy was when her visitor finished talking. She blanched. The boy was Cedric.

25

"So," the stranger said, "have you seen him?"

Lara felt that no good would come out of saying "Yes." She tried hard not to show her surprise. "No," she said.

"Liar," the man hissed quietly. "You lie. I can see it in your eyes."

Damn my eyes, Lara thought. She put on an unfathomable expression. "What makes you think my eyes tell the truth and my mouth does not?" she asked coolly.

The man was startled for a moment. He had not expected her to answer back. His previous interviewees were gullible enough to actually believe that their eyes speak for themselves. When he remained silent, Lara pressed on. "Whose orders are you acting upon?" she asked.

"I serve the king and the king only," the stranger replied coldly.

"Who are *you?*" she asked.

It took the man a long moment to realize what had happened. *What is this wretched girl doing, asking me questions?* he asked himself angrily. "None of your business," he snapped.

He stood and pulled Lara up harshly by the arm, twisting it behind her back. She winced as the pain spread through her arm, starting from the shoulder and ending at the tips of her fingers. The man brought his foul face close to Lara's pretty one. "Where is the Cursebreaker? I know you know, so tell me!" he hissed.

"No," Lara said.

"Well, then you may suffer the consequences!" the man twisted Lara's arm another 180 degrees. She let out a gasp of pain as she felt her arm break. To her horror, her visitor took out a dagger. It had a black hilt and a rusty ivory blade; he held it to her throat. "Tell me, NOW!" the man roared. "Where is he? Where is the Cursebreaker?"

"I—don't—know!" Lara said, gritting her teeth.

"Liar!" he struck her across the face with his gloved hand, which still held the knife. The blade passed over Lara's cheek, leaving a long line of fresh blood behind it; it stung painfully.

The girl stifled a cry of anguish. "You will *never*—be able to find the Cursebreaker—with information from—*me!*" she said, gasping in between every few words.

The man sheathed his dagger and twisted Lara's arm yet again, so that it now made two full rotations. Lara began to cry from the pain. "Please . . . please . . ." she whispered.

Her horrible visitor grinned in satisfaction, threw her roughly to the floor causing her leg to hit the glass table extremely hard, left the inn, mounted his horse, and finally rode away.

26

Lara sat by herself, nursing her broken arm; she felt a bruise forming on her right leg. *I need to go to the healer and then warn Cedric!* she thought desperately.

Lara rose quietly from the floor and went to see the healer. She hoped something could be done for her arm and fast.

*   *   *

"Now, dear," Elvayann said, "it's going to hurt for a long time. You need rest."

Elvayann was the best healer in town. Well, the *only* healer in town. She was a plump woman with a shock of bright red hair that tumbled down to her waist and gray-green eyes. She was kind, but very strict. Elvayann had just finished putting Lara's arm comfortably in a sling. The cut on Lara's cheek was gone and the bruise with it.

Lara glanced down at her arm, which felt considerably better. "Thanks," she said.

"You're welcome, dear," Elvayann murmured, packing or throwing away the medicine bottles and wraps she had used.

"Well, I'll be off, then," Lara said, swinging her legs over the side of the bed on which she had been lying impatiently.

Elvayann quickly looked up. "Did you not hear me?" she asked. "I said you need *rest.*" And with that said, she gently pressed Lara back down on the bed.

"Yeah, well, I need to go somewhere," Lara said testily.

Elvayann's merry eyes had abruptly gone cold. "You are staying here."

"It's *urgent,*" Lara said exasperatedly, getting out of bed.

Elvayann snapped her fingers. Strong ropes were conjured out of thin air and tied Lara back to bed. *Crap,* Lara thought.

"Looks like you'll be staying overnight," Elvayann muttered.

Lara watched the healer walk over to the door to leave, stop, and turn around to face her. "It's for your own good, you know," she said sadly before leaving and locking the door from the outside.

Lara looked around at her surroundings. The white-washed walls were bare, except for a decorated window that looked out into the streets. After listening for a few minutes to make sure that no one was coming. Lara managed to reach inside her boot with her good arm and pull out a switchblade. She then cut the bands that held her together; although it took about five minutes, it felt like an eternity to Lara. The girl stretched her legs and strode over to the window. She opened it and a breeze of fresh air rushed into the room. Lara carefully climbed out of the room and ran to the inn, which was about a block away.

After reaching the stable, which was adjoined to the inn, Lara told the stable boy to get Fireball saddled and ready for a long journey. Fireball was her horse, and he was a fireball, indeed! At sixteen hands high, the horse had a vicious temper. He was a fast steed and was perfect for the job. When Lara had come back from getting provisions, Fireball was ready, stamping his hoof with impatience. His golden coat and mane shone under the afternoon sun.

"Thanks," Lara said to the stable boy as he helped her get on the horse.

"Have a good journey, Miss," he said.

Lara nodded, hoping she would. "G' bye," she told him.

With a squeeze of Lara's legs, Fireball galloped away, out of the city gates of Rotera.

27

Cedric awoke to find the blazing sun glaring at him from the center of the blue, cloudless sky. He sat up and rubbed his eyes and instinctively jumped up at the sound of a familiar scream.

"NOOOO!" Teagen shouted.

Cedric spun around, sword in hand, and saw Teagen thrashing about in her place sleeping, screaming, *and* swearing at the same time. He cautiously sheathed his weapon and dropped down beside the girl, who let out another string of curses.

"NOOOO!" Teagen screamed again. "No, no, no! Never! NEVER!"

"Shh," Cedric said, trying to calm her down and wake her at the same time. "Wake up, Teagen."

Teagen calmed down and stopped screaming, but she was now trembling and still sleeping. With a final shudder, Teagen rolled over and began to snore softly.

Cedric looked at her, stunned. *What's going on?* he wondered.

After fifteen minutes, Teagen woke up and yawned. She was surprised to see Cedric giving her a puzzled look. "What?" she said.

"Y-you were screaming and going c-crazy while you were s-sleeping," Cedric stuttered.

"Oh." Teagen's pretty face clouded over as she frowned. "Really?"

"Yeah. Are you alright?"

"Don't worry. I'm fine. But don't be surprised if it happens again, okay?"

"Yes, but—but *why?*"

"Well," Teagen said as she rose to get some bread for her and Cedric, "it's one of the prices of being a witch."

"Really?"

"Yes. You see, we're haunted with terrible dreams and do and say horrible things while we sleep. Sometimes. The good thing is, though, we don't remember anything that happened during our restless thoughts."

"Can't something be done about it?" Cedric inquired.

Teagen smiled, leaned over, and whispered in his ear, "Some say the Cursebreaker can put an end to this."

28

"The Cursebreaker?" Cedric said in slight amazement.

"But isn't the Cursebreaker supposed to just release Tora from the Curse of Alya?"

Teagen shrugged. "Not really," she said, "but what you heard is probably part of the prophecy."

"There's *more* to the prophecy?"

Teagen nodded. "Yes. You want to hear it?"

"Sure."

The girl closed her eyes for a minute and recited the prophecy:

> The Cursebreaker will lead an army to fight
> To vanquish the darkness and turn on the light.
> He will bring witches' nightmares to an end
> And save his one true love that he worked hard to defend.
> Yet he meets another
> Who forever will treat him as her brother.
> Then one comes along that he hasn't seen in years
> And the sacrifice she makes seduces him to tears.

> Many will live and many will die
> What'll help him is the fact that he can try
> To do what he'll do
> And make it through.
> And the sacrifices that he and others will make
> Will break the curse made on Alya's Lake.

When Teagen finished, she found Cedric looking at her in admiration. "You memorized that?" he asked. "How?"

Teagen grinned shyly. "I was curious about the Cursed Lake of Alya and the prophecy. I guess I memorized it by reading it many times. I still can't make heads or tails of most of it, though."

Cedric sighed and looked at the sun high in the sky. "We really should get going," he said.

They climbed on their mounts and began riding at a steady pace.

29

Both riders thought about the prophecy as they rode.

When they stopped, the moon was shining brightly upon them. They set up their small tents in silence. For some odd reason, Teagen and Cedric did not want to talk; neither of them attempted to engage in a conversation with the other.

Both were immersed in their own thoughts, but not thoughts about the prophecy anymore. Teagen was jealously thinking of Theo and Lorelei, wondering if she'll ever fall in love. Cedric was thinking, yet again, when he should tell Teagen that he loved her. For both of them, it was one of those nights when one wants to sit in their little corner and just think, think about their thoughts and dreams.

That is exactly what Teagen and Cedric did, but instead of corners, they had tents. They thought and thought until they finally fell asleep.

Cedric woke as the sun was rising over the mountains that were barely visible at such a distance. He made sure that both horses were ready and then packed his tent; Teagen was coming out of her own tent, yawning and stretching.

"If we set off now, we should reach Sunset Valley by evening," Cedric told her.

Teagen nodded sleepily and started to dismantle her tent. Cedric went to a nearby creek to fill the empty canteens. When he returned, he heard a loud "Oof!" from Teagen's direction. The tent had collapsed on top of the poor girl and was too heavy for her to push off. Cedric dropped the canteens and rushed over to help. He grinned amusedly as Teagen just stood with a blank look on her face. "Thanks," she mumbled.

"No problem," Cedric said, still grinning, as he heaved the now folded tent onto Zenubia's back. "Let's go."

Teagen, who was still half asleep, and Cedric mounted their horses and rode off to Sunset Valley, where Cedric's past would hopefully be revealed.

30

A sinister plot was in the making once again in King Hsetah's castle. He had called back his assassins, all of who were standing before him, empty-handed. "Since none of you have made progress, I have decided that a simple, yet effective, plan should be devised," he hissed. "I would like to know if you have any ideas, before I waste my precious time thinking."

There was silence from the hired guns until—

"Bait?" an assassin's voice rattled in suggestion.

The king thought for a moment and let out a hiss of satisfaction. "Bait," he murmured. "Yes, bait. But *who* would be the bait?"

Tal answered this question. "How about the girl traveling with the boy? Teagen—I think."

"Teagen?" the king said, startled. "What does she look like?"

As Tal described her, King Hsetah exclaimed, "Have you any idea who she is?"

The assassins looked at each other sheepishly and shook their heads.

"Are you all really that *dense?*" the king cried. "She is the only true heiress of Catéadreâl. Her father, King Perickles, defeated me long, long ago, in a battle in which I was not strong then as I am now. Oh," he hissed in pleasure, "how that would be such *sweet* revenge."

Each of the assassins had the same look of amazement on their faces. They had never heard their master speak of his defeats before.

"What are you all staring at?" King Hsetah roared. "Ride your horses and bring me the girl, the girl *only*. Leave as many clues as possible as to where you are taking her, which is here. I want the boy to follow you here.

Torture the girl as much as you can, but don't be extreme and don't kill her. Leave that to me. Stay together. Now GO!"

With a nod of understanding, the assassins mounted their horses and galloped off to bring Teagen to their master.

31

It was sunrise when Cedric and Teagen reached Sunset Valley. The sun could be barely seen from the teenagers' point of view, but it was still beautiful. The colors could be seen in the Anka River's flowing, clear waters. "We must cross the river and then walk south," Cedric said, recalling Serena's instructions.

"And stop at a bunch of cliffs," Teagen finished. "Well, you go first, being the reason of this trip."

Cedric gave her a shrewd look before giving Tico a nudge. The horse obediently crossed the Anka River without a problem. Zenubia was fine until she got to the middle of the river, when she shied. "Oh, no," Teagen moaned. "Why didn't that stupid horse owner *tell* me she wasn't a river horse?"

"Because he didn't like you?" Cedric teased.

"You shut your—" However, Teagen was cut off when Zenubia bucked and then reared, causing her to fall off. The girl let out a terrific scream that sent some birds in a nearby tree flying away. The last thing she remembered was Cedric grabbing her by her wrist before shrinking into a wave of unconsciousness.

* * *

Cedric, seeing Teagen fall, jumped off Tico and ran to save her. Tico, being a smart horse and sensing what was happening, trotted over to Zenubia, grabbed her reins with his teeth, and dragged her to the bank of the river, where she calmed down. There, they both stood by, watching and waiting for their masters.

Cedric had thrown himself into the water and searched for Teagen. The bubbles clouded his vision; he couldn't see anything for a while until—

His eyes broadened in dread. There was Teagen, floating downwards, unable to move, completely white, and her eyes half-closed. Cedric shot across the water like a torpedo, grabbed Teagen's wrist, and swam to the surface.

Teagen lay limp in Cedric's arms, unconscious. Cedric, on the other hand, was gasping for breath, completely exhausted from the ordeal. Cedric swam to the surface. He stuck his hand into the soft part of the riverbank; the mud felt cool and soggy under his fingers; he knew it wouldn't hold his weight, nonetheless both his and Teagen's. He moved his hand up and clenched the more solid section of the riverbank. Cedric then hoisted Teagen on the grassy mound, where Zenubia dragged the girl by her wet hood. Tico grabbed Cedric by the sleeve and pulled him over to where Teagen lay. "Thanks," Cedric panted, rubbing Tico's forehead.

Cedric sat up, shivering from the icy cold water. He looked at Teagen, whose face was still pale and eyes now closed. He stood and walked over to his horse, which had his bag on his back; he then retrieved some dry clothes and put them on behind a nearby bush. When he finished,

Cedric prepared Teagen's clothes for her, so that she could also change when she regained consciousness.

Cedric looked around at his surroundings. The sun had almost completely risen; the rays bathed everything in sunlight and warmed everything it touched. The land was a grassy, almost flat terrain, with the exception of a few hills and trees here and there. It was quiet, but now the larks began to wake after the owls' midnight hunts; crickets chirped every few seconds, but softly enough so that Cedric could only just hear them. The boy forced himself to turn away from this peaceful moment and focus on Teagen.

Teagen was stirring when Cedric crouched beside her, feeling her pulse. She was freezing, but warmth spread throughout her body when Cedric's warm fingers touched her neck. Teagen opened her eyes and found Cedric's face peering into hers. "You're alive," he said with relief. "Get up and get changed before you get sick."

With that said, Cedric pulled Teagen up by her hand and gave her the dry clothes. "Thank you," she said, shivering.

Teagen clutched the clothes to her chest and found a tall bush to change behind.

32

When Teagen strode out from behind the bush, she found Cedric holding both horses by their halters.

"D'you want to continue?" he asked.

Teagen looked deep into his anxious, blue eyes. She

immediately knew he wanted to go on. "If you want to continue, I'll continue. Wherever you go, I'll go."

Cedric gave the princess a small smile. "Well, since that's settled," he said, getting on Tico, "mount your horse and let's race!"

Teagen grinned; she loved racing. She mounted Zenubia and galloped behind Cedric, who was going south, toward the forest. Zenubia and Tico were neck and neck when, simultaneously, they stopped. There was no word spoken from either rider, who were surprised at the sudden halt and nearly fell head first to the ground. Both horses snorted and pawed the ground with anxiety; their dark eyes were showing white, and their pink nostrils were flaring.

Cedric and Teagen looked around uneasily, trying to see what their horses sensed from the surrounding wood. Both instinctively put a hand to their weapons. They were looking behind them when all of a sudden, there was a big BOOM! and Tico and Zenubia reared.

33

Teagen and Cedric were flung hard off their horses; Zenubia and Tico fled deeper into the forest. Cedric looked up, and his jaw dropped. Standing before him was a massive, greenish-brown, leathery—*thing. What is that?* he wondered as Teagen gasped.

This *thing* was actually an Ostor, a grotesque creature that inhabited the forest. This particular Ostor stood at about fifteen feet in height and looked about seven hundred pounds. It had five bloodshot, puffed up, yellow eyes with bright red irises and orange pupils that continued blinking, giving the impression that it doused and then reignited several fires; these horrifying eyes circled its head. Its nose was wide, and pale-green mucus was dripping from its nostrils. The Ostor's mouth spread into a saliva-dripping, leering grin that showed viciously sharp, decayed, black and yellow teeth that were apart from each other quite a distance. Its pear-shaped head was bald with only a few hairs here and there. The Ostor's large belly hung over its short pants. From its belt hung an axe. Its flat feet were huge with gruesome, brown, infected toenails that were much too long; the hands looked very much like the feet; large and ugly.

Both riders recovered from their fall and, standing up, backed away from the monster. Teagen gripped Cedric's arm in fear; she was extremely tense, for her nails dug into the boy's skin, leaving marks that remained for a full half-hour. "Oh no," she muttered frantically. "Oh no. Oh no, oh no, oh no."

"What *is* this thing?" Cedric hissed.

"It—it's an Ostor," Teagen replied, her voice quavering. "No point in attacking it from behind because it literally has eyes in the back of its head."

"You're joking."

"No, it's the truth."

"What're we going to do?"

"Attack from above."

"Give me a break."

"Only choice."

"That's impossible! We can't fly."

"Any other ideas?"

"Uh . . ."

"Didn't think so."

"Yeah, well it's still impossible!"

"No, it's not!"

While having this quiet argument, Teagen and Cedric did not notice that the Ostor was slowly moving its hand toward the handle of the axe. The sound of the axe being whisked away from the belt was no more than a whisper. Of course, the teenagers didn't hear it, and completely ignored the Ostor. They only realized what it was doing when the blade just missed their heads by millimeters; both ducked and rolled at the same time and unsheathed their swords.

The Ostor let out a roar of anger at missing his prey and lunged, swinging his axe at Teagen and Cedric again. The two dodged the blow. Teagen came up behind Cedric and whispered in his ear, "Distract it."

Cedric nodded and jumped into the air, shouting, "Oy, you ass! Look here!" to divert the creature from concentrating on Teagen; it worked. The Ostor turned its eyes on Cedric as Teagen darted behind a tree.

While Cedric was constantly running from the blows that the monster delivered, Teagen was climbing to the top of a nearby tree with astonishing agility. Then, waiting for the moment to strike, she focused her sword on the monster and crouched on one of the many tree branches. Then, instinctively, Teagen launched herself from her perch. She flew through the air and dug her sword exactly where she intended to plant it: in the middle of the Ostor's head.

34

The Ostor let out a scream of pain. Cedric looked up in amazement to find Teagen trying to jerk her weapon out of the monster's head; she was covered in blood from the waist down. Finally pulling her sword free, Teagen did a flawless back flip and landed lightly on the ground, shouting, "Cedric! Look out!"

The Ostor was swaying dangerously back and forth, all five eyes rolling up into its head and axe swinging around with no specific target. The creature fell forward as Cedric darted to the right, trying to avoid being squashed by the massive body. The axe's blade, still swinging in an ominous manner, sliced through Cedric's elbow. Cedric cried out in agony as he saw half his arm laying a few yards from where he was standing. He clutched what was left of his severed arm. The sight and smell of his own blood overwhelmed him, and he sank to the ground in a faint.

Teagen was horrified at what had just happened. She was ready to vomit when she saw half of her companion's arm just fly through the air like a dead leaf during autumn. She saw Cedric's face when he screamed; it was contorted with pain. Teagen felt terrible; she wanted to turn away, but she knew she couldn't. She was afraid of what would happen to her if she came closer to Cedric, yet she knew she had to help him somehow, someway; he had lost a lot of bloody already. Teagen was so confused. However, when Cedric fainted, she made her decision: she was going to try anything she could to help him stay alive.

35

Cedric opened his eyes a few hours later. He found himself in Teagen's lap, who was rocking him back and forth as a mother would a child. Her eyes were closed and tears were slowly journeying down her pale face. Cedric tried to move his head to see his arm or what was left of it. The movement caused Teagen's eyelids to fly open; she looked down at the boy. "Uh . . . Hi," Cedric said uncomfortably, trying to sit up.

Teagen stared at him with a blank expression and then, bursting into tears, hugged him. "I-I thought y-you d-died," she sobbed. "Y-you l-lost s-so much b-blood. I thought it w-was t-too l-late."

As Teagen sobbed into his shoulder, Cedric glanced at his arm and let out a gasp of surprise; it was completely healed, with no marks on it at all. There was no evidence showing that it was detached hours before. "My arm," he said, "is—"

"Healed," Teagen finished, smiling through her tears. "After you blacked out, I decided to heal your arm by taking the half that came off and rejoining it with the rest of your arm."

"How'd you manage to do that? It's not possible."

Teagen tweaked his nose fondly, saying, "Not if you're a witch. Seeing that I did it already, it's not so impossible anymore, is it?"

Cedric grinned, flexing his fingers. "No, I guess you're right. Thanks. I owe you one."

Teagen waved her hand in the air as if to push the thought aside. "No you don't. You saved my life twice. *I* am the one who is still in debt."

"No need to think of it that way," Cedric murmured,

"but I have to say, I don't think I could ever be more grateful."

"Don't mention it."

As Cedric exercised his re-joined arm, Teagen looked at his handsome profile. She thought about how much they had been through together and smiled. Cedric let out a yawn. "Am-am I hurting you?" he asked coyly, realizing he was still sitting in the girl's lap.

"No, you're not," Teagen replied. "Oh, I forgot. The only reason you're yawning is because of the sleeping spell I had to cast to make sure you didn't wake up in the middle of the 'procedure'. The anesthesia spell might contribute to it, too. It was to make sure the healing process doesn't hurt at all."

"Oh, okay. But, boy, do I feel tired!" he said, struggling to stay awake.

"Lay back," Teagen said gently. When she saw him blushing and resisting to rest in her arms, she said, "Don't be shy. You need to relax if you want your arm to heal properly."

This time, Cedric obediently lay back and rested his head on Teagen's shoulder and immediately fell asleep. Teagen cradled him in her arms, and her heart gave a leap of the utmost joy. She finally found the person she loved. However, the question she wondered before she, too, fell asleep was, did *he* love *her?*

36

A soft breeze woke Teagen up in the middle of the night.
There was something about that breeze, though, that did not seem like the normal, soft wind that would playfully surround and cool a person off. This breeze was warm and smelled of—*grass?* Teagen knew that she and Cedric were in a clearing that was filled with grass, but this aroma was not like the smell of grass that Teagen knew. She opened her eyes and stifled a scream. What scared her was that a pink muzzle was centimeters away from her face. A laugh escaped her lips. Zenubia was nickering softly, as if in apology; Tico was there, too. "Oh, it's so good to see you two," she whispered for fear of waking Cedric up, but there was no point in doing so; Cedric was already sitting up and shouting in surprise. He had not realized that the two horses were standing there.

"Don't—do that—again!" he gasped, still surprised.

Teagen chuckled and stood up as Cedric began shouting at the horses, "Cowards! Absolute cowards! Running away like that! If I have half a mind I would—"

Teagen grabbed Cedric by the shoulders. "Calm down," she said. "They acted as other horses would have acted. They were probably never trained to fight or defend their rider. All they know is how to obey their master. And if I remember correctly, we didn't give any orders when that awful creature attacked, so the horses took matters into their own hands. Or hooves, I should say. You have a whole mind, not a half, not a third. *A whole mind.* Use it."

"I-I didn't think of it that way," Cedric said.

The boy walked over to both horses and stuck his hand out for both of them to sniff. When they came close, he gave them both a hug. "I'm sorry," he whispered.

Tico rested his head on Cedric's shoulder while Zenubia trotted over to Teagen. "Well," Teagen said, already sitting in the saddle, "if you want to see Belle, we'd better continue."

"Right," Cedric said, getting up on his own horse. "Let's go."

37

Teagen and Cedric rode out of the clearing and resumed riding south of where the Ostor still lay. It was only dawn, with the sun's dancing rays just peeking over the mountaintops. A few stars were glistening brightly in the dark blue sky. The full moon was barely visible as some purple clouds lazily drifted past.

After a couple of hours, Teagen asked uncertainly, "Are we lost?"

"I don't know," Cedric responded, just as uncertain.

"What do you mean you 'don't know'? You've got to know!" Teagen exclaimed, her voice sounding shrill.

"Don't panic," Cedric retorted.

"Well, what else am I supposed to do? Am I supposed to just keep on riding, acting like we're not lost and keep my mouth shut or tell you how good a job you're doing, getting us to our destination? Or am I supposed to get off my high horse and do the hula in front of the trees? Go on, tell me! What am I supposed to do, besides panic? What are *we* going to do?"

"I don't know," Cedric said meekly.

"Well, ask for help!"

"What! From who?"

"From him, of course!" Teagen said, pointing upward to what appeared to be—

"A bird? Are you out of your mind? Are you *crazy?* Really, Teagen, I don't think panicking is good for you. You have *got* to be joking, asking a bird for help."

"I'm not. Haven't you ever heard that saying, or whatever it was—you know, when somebody finds something out about another person and the other person asks where he or she heard it from and the answer is something like 'A little bird told me'. Well, it's something like that."

Cedric's head was in a whirlwind. After sorting out what Teagen said, He said, "Yeah, but honestly, Teagen, you're not taking it seriously, are you?"

"Yes, I am. Watch."

Teagen cupped her hands as Cedric shook his head and gave a tremendous shout skyward, "Hey! You up there! Come down here, please!"

Miraculously, the bird sped down to the nearest trees as fast as a bullet and perched itself on the lowest, yet largest branch. Then, in the blink of an eye, the bird transformed into a boy, and hopped down from the branch. "You called me?" the boy asked.

"Yes. What's your name?" Teagen said.

"Septim. Septim's the name."

Septim was a boy about the age of twenty. He had black hair, rosy cheeks, one green eye and one blue eye, and the most jovial smile. He was dressed in a brown T-shirt and dark yellow jeans and boots. Septim had the impressive ability to take the form of a swift hawk within a matter of seconds; not many people in the world could do that, he told Teagen and Cedric.

"Do you know where we can find someone named

Belle?" Cedric asked politely after Septim boasted that he knew every being in the forest.

"Eh—Belle?" Septim thought aloud, scratching his head. "Well, let me think . . . oh yeah! Belle, right. Well, she lives on the other side of the wood. Keep going east and you'll see a lot of cliffs grouped together. She lives somewhere in one of those cliffs."

"Thank you, Septim," Teagen told the boy.

"You're welcome," Septim immediately changed back into a hawk, rose up into the air, and flew out of sight.

"Bye!" Teagen called, after Septim tilted his wings in salute to the two teenagers before disappearing in the clouds.

"Well," Cedric said, also looking at where Septim had vanished. "Shall we get going?"

38

After sometime of riding in silence, Teagen attempted to start a conversation. The girl noticed that Cedric was subdued, and she felt talking would do him some sort of good. "You seem awfully quiet," she said to him.

"I'm just tired, that's all," Cedric murmured.

The sun hung high over their heads. Teagen sighed as she felt the ribbon that held her hair together loosen. She wound Zenubia's reins around the horn of her saddle. Gripping the horse with only her legs, Teagen untied the ribbon and let her hair tumble down to her shoulders.

Cedric glanced at Teagen. He realized she looked different as her hair lolled around her shoulders, gleaming a reddish-gold color in the sunlight. She now looked more like a princess than a runaway. The nobility, pride, and intelligence showed in her beautiful face. Cedric was not paying attention to where he was going, and it resulted in steering Tico into a tree.

"What in the *world* were you looking at?" Teagen asked, trying not to break into a fit of giggles and put her hair up at the same time.

Cedric blushed and mentally reprimanded himself. "Nothing," he said aloud.

Teagen could not help herself; she began to giggle. "Y-you're turning red," she said, letting out a laugh.

Cedric could feel himself getting hot in the face. "I'm sorry," Teagen apologized, "but you just looked so funny, driving the poor horse into an oak. I—oof!"

Teagen had fallen off Zenubia because of laughing so hard; she rolled down the grassy hill on which they were riding. Now it was Cedric's turn to laugh. He got off Tico, and as he was running down the hill to check on Teagen, who was shaking on the ground and hiding her face, tripped on a stone and fell head over heels. Unable to control where he landed, Cedric found himself on top of Teagen, who was still shaking, but with laughter. "I'm sorry," he said, quickly getting up and sitting next to her.

Teagen shook her head and opened her mouth to say something, but instead of words, a snort of laughter escaped her lips. Cedric could not see why she was laughing. "What?" he asked.

"That was *so* much *fun!*" Teagen exclaimed sitting up as well.

Cedric grinned. Then, he lay back, thinking and looking up at the deep blue, cloudless sky. There must have been something in his face that caused Teagen to ask him, "What's wrong?"

"Just thinking," he replied. "Just wondering, what'll happen to me, and you, after we see Belle?"

"Gosh, I didn't even bother to consider that," Teagen murmured. "Well, why don't you put off thinking about it 'til the time comes?"

"The time is nearing," Cedric said, shaking his head. "I have to decide. Soon."

"Don't plan now."

Cedric turned his head and looked at the girl questioningly. "Why?" he asked.

"Belle might say something that could change your plans."

"I guess you're right. Oh! We've been down here long enough. Let's go back to the horses."

Teagen and Cedric stood up and climbed up the hill where their horses were waiting patiently. It was only fifteen minutes since they had rolled down the hill, joyous and carefree. Now, they were somber and quiet, thinking about what the future held for them.

39

It was dusk when Cedric and Teagen rode out of the forest. The moon was rising as the sun was setting. It truly was a magnificent sight. What made it more so was the fact that tiny stars popped up here and there, adding more light to the already illuminated sky.

Just as Septim and Serena had said, a cluster of cliffs was facing them. Cedric dismounted and went up to the massive, rocky structures. There was enough light from the lit up sky to help Cedric make out the minuscule words etched in stone. "Katé fàre chaté," he murmured, reading aloud.

The earth under him suddenly began to rumble and quake. There was a loud ripping noise, and the cliff that stood before Cedric suddenly had a long crack in it. The crack grew wider and wider until it was broad enough to walk through.

Cedric turned to Teagen who was gaping in amazement. He gestured to her. "Leave the horses," he told her.

Teagen nodded and dismounted, gazing uneasily at the dark walkway that the crack in the cliff provided. She tied the nervous horse to a nearby tree. Coming up behind Cedric, she whispered, "I never thought I would admit this to anyone, Cedric, but I'm scared."

"Me, too, but I think we're safe going in," he whispered back, "I mean, I don't think Serena would send us to an unsafe place."

"Are you sure?"

"Not a hundred percent, but I'll be sure of *something* once we go in. Are you ready?"

Teagen tore her gaze away from the breach in the cliff and focused her steady brown eyes on Cedric's blue ones. "With you," she told him, "I'll be ready for anything."

Cedric smiled, and advancing forward with Teagen by his side, walked into the deep, dark unknown that was beckoning to him.

40

There was another loud noise as the entrance closed behind Cedric and Teagen, engulfing the two in complete darkness. The ceiling of the dark, damp, winding tunnel that they were walking through served as a home for large creatures that resembled bats. As one flew right above her head, Teagen let out a shriek and groped for Cedric's hand in the gloom.

Cedric, sensing Teagen's panic, found the girl's hand and held it tightly. Since he could still feel her trembling about ten minutes after he took her hand, he put his arm round her waist and drew her close to him; Teagen stopped shaking almost immediately.

Teagen was thoroughly afraid of this unknown tunnel that she found herself walking in. Even when Cedric held her hand, she could not keep from quaking. However, when he pulled her close to him, all of Teagen's fears left her. For some unexplained reason, the girl felt a happiness like no other. She felt light and positive; she felt joyful to the point of tears. Teagen smiled in the dark.

After another fifteen minutes of walking, the two came up to an oak door; it was clearly seen as a result of a lighted torch on either side of the door. The door stretched from floor to ceiling and was as wide as the tunnel itself. However—

"There's no doorknob," Cedric observed.

"Look," Teagen whispered, pointing to a sign next to the door; it appeared to be written in blood.

The sign, written on a piece of broken wood said:

> Knock mortal, if you dare
> Beware the consequences; beware! Beware!
> Beyond this door lie answers to what you ask

> But answer this,
> Has thou completed thy task?
> Your answer lies within the center
> Answer correctly and you can enter
> Speak your answer, but no other word
> Otherwise, that'll be the last sound heard!

Teagen and Cedric looked at each other, chills running up an down their spines. Cedric pointed to the line that said, "Your answer lies within the center," and gave Teagen a questioning look.

Teagen had such a look of concentration on her face that Cedric was sure that she was going to burst. Then, the girl smiled. She pointed at three letters in the question, "Hast thou completed thy task?"; y-e-s. Teagen mouthed to Cedric, "Say 'yes'!"

Cedric grinned in understanding and said aloud, "Yes!"

41

The sign next to the door now read, "ENTER" in a welcoming bright-green color. The door began to slowly move downward, as if someone was pushing a card into a slot. While waiting for the door to completely sink into the ground, Cedric looked appreciatively at Teagen and said, "What would I ever do without you?"

"Fail," Teagen teased.

Teagen put her hand on her hip and realized that Cedric was still holding her. She took his hand and squeezed it, saying, "The question really is, what would *I* do without *you?*"

"Die of fear," Cedric said, grinning.

Teagen laughed. "Probably."

By now, the door had disappeared, and the two stepped inside. Cedric nervously put his hands inside his pockets and gazed at his surroundings.

The room they were in was very large and lavishly furnished. Its wall were a deep purple hue. The sofas were also purple, but with bright white stars. The pillow cushions were a pacific blue. There were four brown, round tables, three of which had pictures on them. The fourth was in a corner with two chairs on opposite sides. The table had a blue cover that was decorated with more stars. In the middle of the table sat a foggy, crystal ball. Another doorway was at the other end of the room; it had a curtain of beads, which blocked anyone from seeing what's going on inside the room. The carpet spread out over the rocky, earthen floor was bedecked with yellow moons and stars.

Teagen and Cedric looked at some of the pictures on the table. "That man sort of looks like you, Cedric," Teagen murmured, pointing at a picture of a young man with a smiling face, round blue eyes, and ruffled chestnut hair. It was in a frame that was a soft shade of green.

"Skies above," Cedric breathed. He staggered backward. The boy was pale and his eyes wide in astonishment.

"Cedric!" Teagen cried. "What on earth is the matter?"

"Th-that man," the boy whispered, "*is* my father."

42

"Your father?" Teagen gasped. "Are you sure?"

"Sure, I'm sure," Cedric said, tears streaming down his face. "I'd recognize him anywhere. You said so yourself, we even look alike."

"She wouldn't happen to be your mother, would she?" Teagen asked uncertainly, pointing at another picture. This one was of a female elf. She had slanted, brown eyes; pointy ears; high cheekbones; a petit nose; and a slightly round face. This frame was pink.

More tears came down Cedric's face. "Yeah, she is," Cedric said.

Cedric looked at another photo. It showed a little boy about a year old. He had twinkling blue eyes, chestnut-colored hair, and a one-tooth smile; it was in a turquoise frame. "Hey! This is me!" he cried out. "Where'd she get all these pictures from?"

"We'll find out soon," Teagen replied. "HELLO? IS ANYBODY HOME?" she shouted.

"Yes. I am," said a weary, yet clear voice from behind them as Teagen and Cedric spun around.

43

A girl of about nineteen stood in the beaded doorway. She was tall and slim. She had a round face and wide, round, brown eyes; her plaited, blonde-brown hair went down right below her waist. The girl wore a colorful v-necked dress that went down to the middle of her thighs over black, tight pants. She wore black boots that were similar to Teagen's, but instead had three silver buckles. "I am Belle," she said quietly. "Whom do I owe the pleasure of meeting?"

"Teagen," muttered Teagen, looking at the floor.

"Greetings, princess."

Teagen looked up sharply, saying, "How'd you—"

"You have already forgotten who I am," Belle said, giving them a wry smile. "And you are . . . ?"

"Cedric," came the answer grudgingly.

"Cedric? Not the little boy in the picture over there?" Belle said in slight surprise, pointing to the picture of the little boy.

"Just so happens that the answer to your question is yes," said Cedric angrily. "But I want to know this, where'd you get all these pictures of me, my mother, and my father?"

"You don't know?" Belle asked as her face fell.

"D'you know what?" Cedric said, his voice rising. "I come here to get one or two simple questions answered, but instead, more issues begin to arise! And do you know what that means? MORE QUESTIONS!" he roared.

"Cedric, calm down," Teagen whispered anxiously, putting her hand on his arm. "Let Belle explain. I'm sure she has a good reason for all this."

"Indeed, I do," Belle murmured, wiping the look of doubt off of Teagen's face. "Please, sit down, and I'll explain everything."

"So," Belle told Cedric, "Mother and Father never told you that I was your sister?"

44

Silence. Teagen had an incredulous look on her face.

Cedric, on the other hand, looked at Belle blankly and said, "What?"

"I said—" Belle began.

"Oh, I heard what you said," Cedric rudely interrupted, his brow furrowing, "but do you mean to tell me that I went sixteen years without *anybody* telling me I had a sister?"

"Possibly," Belle said quietly.

"All right, I've had enough of this," Cedric said, getting up and walking over to the other side of the room.

"He can be a little—uh—*impatient* at times," Teagen explained in an undertone to a bewildered Belle. "If you'll excuse me."

Teagen arose from the sofa and Belle said, "If you'd like to talk in the other room, help yourself."

"Thank you," Teagen said, giving Belle a small smile.

Teagen walked over to where Cedric was standing; his back was to her. Teagen gently touched the boy's shoulder, and he spun around. "What?" he said irritably.

Teagen then took his hand and whispered, "Come."

With the girl holding his hand in a vise-like grip, Cedric had no other choice but to obey. Teagen led him into the room with the beaded doorway.

This room was smaller, and it had light-green walls. There was a bed, a table, and a small, plushy couch. There was also another doorway, except it had a curtain, instead of beads or a door. Teagen led Cedric to the couch; they sat down. "What's wrong, Cedric?"

"I-I can't believe it," Cedric said, his head in his hands, his shoulders shaking. "I just can't."

Teagen put her arms around the boy's broad shoulders. "It's not that you *can't* believe it, it's that you don't *want* to believe it."

Cedric shook his head. "You wouldn't understand," he muttered.

"Fine, I might not," Teagen said slowly. "But won't it be a good thing that you found your long-lost sister? That you finally found a relative; your own flesh and blood?"

When Cedric didn't say anything. Teagen continued, "You could always spend time with her, instead of—of living alone." She hesitated at the last few words as a thought washed over her.

The girl had realized something. *If Cedric* did *end up spending a lot of time with Belle,* she thought, *he might forget about me!* Then, Teagen caught herself. *I mustn't think that way.*

Teagen gave Cedric a hug. "Go and apologize to Belle," she said, "and listen to her story."

"Alright," Cedric said resignedly, getting up.

The boy left the room with Teagen right behind him.

45

Belle had been lost in thought while Teagen and Cedric were talking in the other room. She looked up when they returned. With an encouraging nod from Teagen, Cedric apologized. Belle smiled and said, "It's okay. I completely understand. Please, sit down and let me explain everything."

Once the two sat down, Belle began her story. "Oh, let's see," she murmured. " 'Twas about fifteen years ago, when I was four years old and you were one, Cedric. A mysterious woman had visited us. Mother and Father didn't know her well. All they knew was that she was a revered fortune-teller and that she was to be respected.

"On the night before the morn that she was to leave, she told Mother and Father that she felt that I was gifted in the arts of 'Telling', I think was what she called it. She begged our parents to take me and train me. She said I would become greater than any fortune-teller that ever lived."

"How so?" Teagen asked curiously.

Belle smiled, remembering. "That's exactly what Mother asked. Madame Lundi—that was the lady's name—said I was blessed with the knowledge of anyone's past *and* future. Usually, fortune-tellers know a person's future.

"After many hours of pleading. Mother and Father gave in to Madame Lundi. Mother gave me those pictures you see over there before I left.

"And so, Madame Lundi and I were on our way the next day. As two horses dragged the caravan we were traveling in, Madame began to teach me all she knew about fortune telling. I missed home more and more as the days slowly passed. I still do today. But I had such a jolly time, though, seeing new places and learning new things.

"Regrettably, about three weeks into our journey, Madame Lundi passed away. However, right before she died, she gave me instructions on how to get here. And here I am."

"So you really are my sister?" Cedric said, his voice cracking with uncertainty.

"Yes."

"Are you sure?"

"Yes."

"Positive?"

Teagen rolled her eyes as Belle laughed. "Yes, brother, I am your sister. I am sure as I am positive that Teagen is sitting next to you."

Cedric yawned as he said, "I-I b-be-believe y-you."

"Oh dear," Belle said. "I bet you're both tired from your journey. You two can have the other room, but one of you will have to sleep on the couch!"

Teagen grinned; she and Cedric arose from the sofa. Belle got up, too, and asked Cedric teasingly, "Do you think I could give my little brother a good-night hug?"

Cedric smiled and gave his sister a hug. Teagen was so happy for them both that she almost cried as she stood in the background. With one last "Good-night" to Belle, Cedric and Teagen walked into the other room and went to sleep.

46

Or tried to. Cedric fell asleep before his head hit the soft pillow. Teagen, on the other hand, couldn't go to sleep; she needed to talk to someone.

Back at the castle in Catéadreâl, Teagen's mother, Queen Chloe, was always available for her daughter. Whenever Teagen had a problem or just wanted to talk, Queen Chloe listened. But here, many miles from home where her mother was, Teagen felt lost. The girl desperately needed someone to talk to. *Definitely not Cedric,* she thought. *He's not the right person. I know! Belle! I just hope she's awake.*

Teagen quickly left the softness of the plush couch and quietly went to the sitting room.

Belle was waiting for her, sitting on a sofa, wide awake. "I knew you wanted somebody to talk to, so I stayed here. What do you want to talk about?"

Teagen collapsed on the opposite sofa. "I thought you knew," she joked.

Belle smiled, but her eyes were serious. "It'd be better if you talked. Then, you could relieve yourself from the weight on your back."

"Too true," Teagen muttered, fidgeting uncomfortably. "Well—er—I, um, don't know how to put it—but, um—"

"Spit it out," Belle said, not unkindly.

"I'm in love with Cedric," Teagen said quickly, looking at the floor.

"You are?"

"You're not angry with me, are you?" Teagen asked tentatively, looking at Belle.

"Good heavens, no!" Belle chortled. "It's absolutely wonderful!"

"Yes, but I—"

"Don't know when to tell him?"

"Yes."

Belle leaned forward and said gently, "Only time will tell. Be patient. Your future will unfold. Remember, Teagen, there is *always* a right time for everything and everyone."

Teagen nodded. "Thank you so much, Belle."

"You're welcome. G'Night."

"Night."

Teagen rose from the sofa and walked into the bedroom and immediately fell asleep on the sofa, warm couch, not restless anymore. For now.

47

"C'mon, Fireball, go faster!" Lara urged her horse.

Fireball put on a new burst of speed. Foam had gathered around the corner of the horse's mouth. The wind whipped Fireball's mane back and Lara's face with such force that was never felt before until now; it made Lara wonder how fast Fireball could really go. Lara almost enjoyed the ride, but then remembered her errand.

It was dawn, and Lara was coming out of the same wood that Cedric and Teagen had come out of the day before. "Halt!" she cried. Fireball obediently stopped, panting from his long, hard run. Lara saw two horses, one of which she recognized as Tico, and knew that she had come to the right place.

Dismounting, the girl tied Fireball securely to a nearby tree and gave him some water. When the horse finished, she ran over to the great wall of rock and searched for the words in the Forgotten Language that Teagen had told her about; Lara finally found them and said the words out loud. After experiencing the same phenomenon that Cedric and Teagen had encountered, Lara walked inside the cliff and fearlessly ran down the long, dark tunnel. She finally came upon the large door and the wooden sign.

* * *

"Rise and shine!" Belle said cheerfully, waking up a sleepy Teagen and a well-rested Cedric. "Breakfast's ready!"

Teagen rubbed her eyes as Cedric followed Belle out of the room. She, too, lumbered out of the room after a few quiet minutes of staring into space. She arrived just in time to hear Cedric eagerly ask, "Do you know how Mother and Father died and what my future's going to be like?"

Belle shook her head at her brother's eagerness and sighed as she handed Cedric and Teagen each a plate of eggs. "Cedric, all I will tell you right now is that, although your past was bleak, you have such a bright future ahead of you."

As she said this, all three heard the soft chime of bells. The ringing was so serene and harmonious; it was almost like a quiet lullaby. "What are the bells for?"

"The bells ring when someone is at the door," Belle explained. "I sense we have an anxious visitor at that."

Belle was right. She sighed. "This is the fastest the darned door will ever go." The door was going down at its usual slow pace, but the person on the other side apparently didn't think it was fast enough. The visitor kept on pounding impatiently on the door.

"Some people just *have* to learn how to wait," Teagen grumbled in disgust.

Imagine her surprise when she saw Lara standing in the doorway, face flushed, out of breath, wisps of blonde hair coming out of her usually neat ponytail, and arm in a sling.

48

"Come in," Belle said after a moment's silence.

"Thank you," Lara gasped, stepping into the coolness of the room.

"Lara!" Teagen cried.

"Lara? Where?" Cedric asked, looking up from his breakfast. "Oh," he said sheepishly. "Hi."

"Hello, Cedric," Lara said breathlessly. She turned to Belle. "Are you Belle?" she asked hesitantly, noticing the stern look in Belle's eyes.

"Why, yes, I am," Belle said in mild surprise.

"Please forgive me for entering your home this way. I'm sorry, but I *must* speak to Cedric. It's urgent."

"Of course," Belle said graciously.

"What'd 'oo wanna tell 'e?" Cedric asked with his mouth full of eggs.

"Don't talk with your mouth full," Belle scolded.

"Alright, alright," the boy said angrily, gulping he last of his breakfast. "So," he said turning to Lara, "what'd you want to talk to me about?"

"Y-you have to hide," Lara said, her voice faltering for the first time since she arrived.

"Why?"

"You don't know?"

"Oh, here we go again! Honestly, I reckon you three lasses are teaming up against me with all this 'you don't know' business. Wait, let me guess," Cedric said mockingly, before Lara could even open her mouth. "You are my . . . wait, wait, wait . . . er—I know! You're my cousin, aren't you?"

"What on *earth* is he talking about?" Lara asked incredulously, looking from Teagen to Belle.

"*You don't know?*" Cedric said in mock surprise.

"He's gotten drunk off life." Teagen whispered to Lara, rolling her eyes and giggling.

"Ah . . ." Lara murmured. Turning to Cedric with a straight face, she told him. "Life's booze ain't good for a lad your age."

"What—Oh ho!" Cedric exclaimed. "Teasing me, are you? Well, you know what? You can—"

"Okay, okay," Belle said, raising her voice, feeling this was taking a wrong turn. "Lara, what did you want to tell Cedric? I think now would be a good time to tell him."

"Oh, right," Lara said, a little embarrassed.

"Sit down, please," Belle said. "I've got a feeling it's going to be a *long* story."

49

Once everyone was seated, Lara told her story of the mysterious visitor she had and how she figured out that Cedric was the Cursebreaker and that the king was looking for him. There was an awkward silence when the girl was done. Cedric broke the silence, "Did you know?" he asked Belle quietly.

Belle sighed heavily. "Yes, I did," she said.

"This has gotten too much for me. I-I think I'll go to bed." With that said, Cedric rose from his seat and went to his bedroom.

"What's wrong with him?" Lara inquired. "He seems so—depressed."

"Who can blame him?" Belle said. "After what he found out today and yesterday, I don't think he can hold it in any longer."

"What'd he find out?"

"That she's his sister," Teagen murmured, nodding at Belle.

"Well, isn't that—*good?*" Lara asked.

Belle shook her head. "Alas, no. You see, he's been on

his own for such a long time, and he has grown independent. I think that he's afraid he'll lose his independence while I'm around—you know, telling him what to do and what not to do—and, at the same time, feel pressured with the responsibilities and tasks of being the Cursebreaker."

"But how does he know what he's going to do if he just found out that he's the Cursebreaker?"

Belle thought for a moment. "You know, that's a good question. I wonder, as well."

"I told him the full prophecy," Teagen said guiltily, "while we were traveling."

"Well," Belle said, "what is done is done. There is nothing we can do about the past. We shouldn't worry about the future until the time comes, either. We must focus on what is occurring in the present. Now. We must always live in the present and not in the past or future."

Teagen stood up. "I think I'm going to check on the poor boy and make sure he doesn't kill himself."

"Geez," Lara said, "is it that bad?"

"You have no idea," Teagen replied. "Cedric can be unpredictable at times. This may be one of those times."

50

Teagen found Cedric sitting on the bed, head in his hands, and shoulders shaking; he was crying. "Cedric?" Teagen said softly.

The boy continued to cry noiselessly, giving no sign that he heard her. Teagen sat down next to him. "Cedric," she said, "talk to me."

Cedric shook his head. Teagen sighed. "Please," she pleaded. "Please, talk to me."

He stubbornly shook his head again. Fed up, Teagen took his face in her hands and raised his head so that his tear-filled eyes were level with hers. "Cedric," she repeated, *"I want you to talk to me.* What is wrong?"

The boy took a deep breath. "What'm I g-gonna do?" he whispered, mortified. "If I *am* the Cursebreaker, so many people will depend on me. What do I do, Teagen? What do I do?"

Cedric's blue eyes were wide and bright with tears. He looked at the girl desperately, as if she held the answer. Teagen put her arms around the boy. "I don't know," she said sadly. "But what I *do* know is that I'll always be there to help you."

The two sat in silence for a while. "Teagen?" Cedric said suddenly.

"Hm?"

"Thanks."

"For what?"

"For everything."

"You're welcome, Cedric."

51

Lara walked into the room that Teagen and Cedric were in.

"Teagen," she began, "what's taking you s—?"

She stopped short and quietly backtracked out of the room.

* * *

Teagen awoke with a start; she realized that she had been sleeping, sitting up, for what felt like several hours. Her shoulder was aching, but she didn't know why. She turned her head and found Cedric's head resting peacefully on her shoulder. He was pale, though, and his mouth was slightly hanging open. Teagen gently shook her shoulder, but it was enough to wake Cedric up. "Your mouth seemed like the perfect place for a fly to rest," she joked.

Cedric did not share the girl's humor. On the contrary, actually; he looked miserable as he stared at the floor. "What am I ever going to do with you?" Teagen sighed.

"I don't know, but I know what I'm going to do with me," Cedric said quietly. "I'm going to kill myself."

Teagen looked horrified. "Oh, Cedric you mustn't do that . . . Please . . . There are loads of people who'll help you through this and who will follow you and be part of your army. It's not the end of the world."

Cedric laughed harshly. "Oh yeah? Like who?"

"Belle . . . Lara . . . me . . ."

"Oh, yes," Cedric said sarcastically. "Three people in my army. What a lot of good that'll do. Hey! Let the three of us go and kill the king right now, before he gets me!" He laughed callously again; it was a laugh that Teagen wasn't familiar with. It wasn't his sweet, musical laugh. It just wasn't. But this fact didn't daunt her from giving him the support he needed at that moment.

"It's a start," she said.

Cedric stopped laughing. "You know what? I'll put this all behind me," Cedric muttered, crossing over to the other side of the room. He picked up his sword, which was leaning on the wall, and unsheathed it, the blade glinting ominously in the lamplight.

Teagen stood up, looking alarmed. "Cedric," she said desperately, walking over to him. "You're not going to—?"

"Yeah, I am. The world's better off without me."

"Cedric, you were put in this world for a reason. You have a purpose. Everybody does."

"Teagen, we both know I'm going to fail."

"No, you're not! Cedric, there are people who'll always be by your side—"

"No, there won't be!" Cedric was now on the verge of tears. "I remember my parents telling me the same exact thing—they're not here, now, are they?"

"Well, it won't do any good at all if you kill yourself!" Teagen said firmly, placing her hands on the sword's blade.

"It won't do any good if I didn't."

"Yes it would!"

"Nobody cares, Teagen. Nobody." Cedric said quietly.

"That's not true. People have been waiting for you for a long time. You're their only hope left to leading a peaceful, fear-free life. Besides, there are people who care about you and love you."

"Who? Tell me, Teagen. Who?"

"Belle."

"I just met her. How do I know if she isn't going to betray me to the king? She's a stranger to me, even though she's my sister. Excuse me; even though she *says* she's my sister. Go on. You said there were *people,* not a *person.*"

"Erm . . ."

"So you can't think of anybody else." It was more of a challenge than a simple statement. Teagen's next words tumbled out of her mouth before she knew what she was saying. "What about me?"

Cedric looked taken aback. "What?"

"Me, Cedric. Me. I admit it. I love you."

Cedric looked suspiciously at the girl. "I think—"

But Cedric never finished saying what he thought. Teagen had suddenly wound her arms around his neck and put her mouth on his in a passionate kiss. Cedric dropped the sword and fell to the floor with a clang. He wrapped his arms around her waist, and the two stood together, lips locked, for several long minutes. Whether they were minutes or hours, Cedric couldn't tell. He felt the love pulsing between them, emanating from that one kiss. He felt Teagen move ever closer so that there bodies were now touching. Cedric held her even tighter. His heart was throbbing; he knew. He loved her and she loved him back. Cedric tore away for a moment and looked into Teagen's dancing eyes. "So you *do*—"

The boy was interrupted once again, but this time by two piercing, feminine screams.

"Belle and Lara!" Teagen exclaimed.

With one swift motion, Cedric picked up his sword and ran out of the room with Teagen at his heels. A shocking scene met their eyes. Seven black-clothed figures were standing in the sitting room, weapons drawn, and were cornering Belle and Lara.

"Oy!" Teagen exclaimed angrily. "You stupid idiots, leave my friends alone!"

The strangers turned around with surprise. One of them allowed a rattle to escape from his mouth and, pointing at Teagen, said, "*Get her.*"

Cedric defiantly stepped in front of Teagen, raised his sword, and slashed at one of the advancing figures. To his surprise and disappointment, his blade went through, but did not cause any harm.

With a taunting laugh, the creature slapped Cedric

across the face and sent the boy flying into a wall. Then, he grabbed Teagen by the wrist and dragged her out of the room and into the tunnel from which they had entered. However, Teagen did not go without a fight: she bit, kicked, and hit; yet she did not inflict any damage upon the kidnappers. Before she was dragged out, Teagen desperately cried out to the boy who sagged unconscious against the wall, "Cedric! Help me!"

As all six beings victoriously marched out of the room bearing Teagen, one lingered behind in the room. He was examining the sword that Cedric still grasped. He let out a hiss of dismay when he read the minuscule words inscribed in the blade: "The Sword of Damaé."

After casting a worried glance at the boy, the figure stalked out of the room after his evil companions.

52

Cedric slowly opened his eyes and looked up at what appeared to be a starry night sky. He then realized it was Belle's ceiling *made* to look like the sky. He tried to remember what had happened, and the unfortunate events rushed back to him. Only three words now registered in his brain: *Must. Find. Teagen.*

Suddenly, a shadow loomed over him, a recognizable shadow. Belle's shadow. "Oh, brother, I'm so glad you're all right!" she exclaimed.

Cedric sat up and shook his head. Both Belle and Lara looked tired and nervous, but relieved all the same. "Who were they?" Cedric asked hoarsely, referring to Teagen's kidnappers.

"They call themselves the Surrendered Seven," Belle responded quietly.

"That helps," Lara said with a trace of sarcasm in her voice.

"But what do they do?" Cedric muttered, ignoring Lara's comment.

"They serve King Hsetah," Belle said in a grave voice as Lara let out a gasp and Cedric looked up somberly. "They are seven beings having surrendered themselves, including their souls to him, hence the name 'Surrendered Seven'. They don't do anything except obey their master."

"How come I couldn't kill them?" Cedric inquired curiously.

"The Surrendered Seven are close to being invincible. They could be killed once the king is dead."

"But why did they take Teagen? Why didn't they take me? It's me they want, right?" Cedric said more to himself than to Belle.

"I-I don't know why they took her, Cedric," Belle said sadly.

Cedric looked down at the floor. "Teagen told me that she loved me. Just before she—she—" He couldn't bring himself to finish his sentence.

"Not surprised," Lara muttered, while Belle said nothing at all.

The boy deducted something from Belle's silence. He looked up at her. "You knew, didn't you?"

Belle gave her brother a cheerless smile. "She told me last night."

Cedric abruptly stood up. "I've got to find her," he announced. "Now."

Striding over to the other side of the room, he picked

up his fallen sword and sheathed it. "Let me come with you," Lara said from behind him.

The boy turned around. "No. It'll be too dangerous."

"I don't care. I'm coming."

"No, you're not," Cedric said, raising his voice.

"Yes, I am. She's my friend just as much as yours!" Lara hollered.

Cedric shook his head and glared at Lara. She didn't understand. Teagen wasn't just a friend to him. She was his love. His companion. He wanted to be alone when he found Teagen and tell her how much he loved her.

When Lara opened her mouth to argue, Belle put a hand on her arm and gave the girl a warning look; Lara closed her mouth. *Thank you, Belle!* Cedric thought gratefully.

"Why don't we just go outside and see the boy off?" Belle suggested smoothly.

Lara calmed down enough to say, "Fine."

The trio went outside the cliff to where the three horses were waiting patiently for their masters.

Or two.

Cedric immediately realized that Zenubia was gone; he looked inquiringly at Belle. The girl took in the scene of a cut rope wrapped around a tree and a number of hoof marks surrounding it. "They have taken Zenubia, as well," she observed.

"Why?" Lara whispered.

"Because, since they have only seven horses—one for each of them—and Teagen makes eight travelers—another horse was needed," Belle correctly surmised.

"This is not good," Cedric said, shaking his head. "I must go before it's too late."

"Well, seeing as I can't go," Lara muttered grudgingly, "you can take Fireball, since he's loads faster than Tico."

"Thank you, Lara," Cedric said while giving Tico a hug. His horse let out a soft snort.

Cedric sighed sadly as he mounted Fireball. On the horse, Cedric looked noble, yet grave. With his arrows in a cylindrical case strapped on his back, his bow slung over his shoulder, and the Sword of Damaé attached to his belt, he looked almost kingly.

"Farewell, my brother," Belle said, her eyes filled with grief. "And though fate must separate us once again, remember that my love is with you. Always."

"My sister, I cannot be more grateful to you than I am now," Cedric said with a heavy heart.

"Well, good-bye," Lara said glumly.

"Good-bye to you, too."

Just as Cedric was about to leave, Belle gave a cry of shock. "Oh my goodness!" she exclaimed, pointing.

Cedric turned Fireball around in the direction that Belle was pointing and let out a gasp at the same time as Lara did. To his amazement, a small hawk came trundling out of the forest. The animal looked terribly familiar . . . those yellow legs . . . brown feathers . . . "Septim!" Cedric suddenly shouted.

Belle muttered a few words and the hawk slowly turned into a boy who lay unconscious on the ground. The girl then revived Septim; the poor boy's eyes slid in and out of focus, and he was muttering nonsense words under his breath. Belle finally looked at her brother. "You know him?" she asked, surprised.

"Yes," Cedric replied. "Teagen and I asked him for directions to here and—"

"MOM, COME BACK!" Septim screamed suddenly.

"What the bloody hell is wrong with him?" Lara asked incredulously.

"Tortured into insanity by the Surrendered Seven," Belle answered grimly. "That's how they knew you and Teagen were here, Cedric. And, by the looks of it, they went pretty far before they got what they wanted."

"So they tortured him to get information out of him?" Lara asked quietly.

"Yes."

Cedric became even more resolute in his search for Teagen. "I can't imagine what they'll do to Teagen if they made Septim insane just for a bit of information," he said. "Now I really must go!"

"Take care . . ." Lara said.

". . . And beware," Belle finished.

Cedric nodded to both of them. "You, too."

Then, with a last look at Septim, he turned Fireball around and sped directly into the forest.

53

Teagen found herself in an extremely uncomfortable, yet familiar situation. She sat on Zenubia, with a long, thin, spiked pole stuck in the hole in her saddle, her hands bound to it and bloody from the sharp points; she also had a nasty tasting gag in her mouth. However, unlike the position she was in before, in which her royal guards captured her, her captors were queer creatures. They resembled men, yet they were not. For one thing, when they spoke, their words were mingled with a rattling sound; another thing was that they could not be harmed with a sword blade, which astounded her.

At that moment, Teagen was emitting loud squeaks from behind the piece of nasty cloth stuffed into her mouth. It was gagging her; at any moment, she would throw up. "Could someone shut that human UP!" growled one of the creatures.

"We could, Zake, but the question is *will* we and *how*," muttered another.

"Don't be smart, Tal," Zake snarled.

"You know, this human seems to be a bit off color!" exclaimed one of the creatures, this one particularly overweight.

"You're right, Refe," said Lakt, another member of the group. "Look at that greenish color that she's slowly taking on . . ."

It was true. Teagen felt herself choking, her breakfast leaving her stomach and slowly creeping up towards her throat. She began to break into a sweat.

"I understand that humans release liquid from somewhere below their waists. It's called urinating or peeing," said Het, the so-called smartest of the Surrendered Seven. "However, according to my keen observations, this human seems to be abnormal. Look! she's peeing from her face!"

Ako and Leus, the youngest of the bunch, peered intently at the small beads of sweat that were forming on Teagen's forehead. Their horrible stench of decaying bodies was too much for Teagen to handle. She finally let out a stifled hiccup and vomit began to seep through the cloth. "Oh, ugh!" exclaimed Leus, quickly pulling back, along with Ako.

"Somebody, quick! Untie the cloth!" shouted Zake. However, everyone seemed reluctant to do so.

"Shouldn't we be torturing her, though?" Refe asked hesitantly.

"Yeah, boss. Ain't this torture?" said Ako.

"You idiots!" spat Zake. "You don't want to put up with that nasty smell she's making with whatever's coming out of her mouth, do you? Het, take off the cloth!"

"Aw, why me, boss? Why not somebody else?" whined Het.

"Because I said so, you son of a tree stump!" roared Zake. "Now do it!"

Still grumbling, Het untied the cloth. Teagen threw her head to one side to avoid spewing her breakfast all over Zenubia and threw up on what she hoped was the ground; instead, it went all over Het and his horse's saddle. Furious, Het slapped Teagen across the face. "How *dare* you!" he screeched. "How dare you throw up on this saddle and me! You threw up on me, the most wonderful, perfect, hard-working, handsomest—"

"Didn't your mother ever tell you not to lie?" asked Refe with a straight face.

"And didn't *your* mother ever tell you not to raid the fridge?" countered Het.

"Why, you little—"

"Now, now, boys. No fighting. It's not polite to fight in front of guests. Didn't your mother ever teach you *that?*" Zake said lazily.

"Guest? Guest?" Het said incredulously. "We're not supposed to treat her like a *guest*. We're supposed to torture her!"

"Yes, yes, I know," murmured Zake. "But she's our guest for tonight's Firedance."

"Ooo," whispered Ako and Leus.

54

Cedric was hot on the trail the Surrendered Seven left behind. He wondered where they were taking Teagen. He knew close to nothing about the group.

Cedric stopped to rest; he had been out of the forest for a long time now. He had come this far without any trouble. Cedric looked around uneasily. This was a desolate area. The land was dry and brown with some brush here and there. There were a few trees, as well.

Cedric felt something was wrong. *I'm just being paranoid,* he thought as a crow let out a caw in a nearby tree. But still . . . coming so far . . . no trouble . . . This was *way* too easy. Cedric thought hard for a long time. Fireball seemed fine. He might as well just go to sleep. He still felt unsure about sleeping out in the open; he was vulnerable. Cedric fell into a restless sleep, one filled with terrible nightmares and dreadful visions.

55

Teagen was horrified. She was still stuck to the pole, and the group had recently tied her feet to the metal stick.

Only now, instead of sitting on her saddle, she was amidst sticks and stones. When she heard the word "Firedance," she had no idea what it meant, except that it sounded menacing.

The leader, Zake, stood before her leering. He muttered, "Feu resvel." Teagen recognized it as magic. He had said, "Fire arise."

What am I going to do now? Teagen thought.

She realized that this was torture. Teagen hoped they wouldn't kill her, but she wouldn't have put it past them.

Magic words ... She knew they were magic ... Magic! Of course! She could use *magic* to protect herself. *Why didn't I think of it sooner?* she wondered, marveling at her own stupidity.

All of a sudden, she began to feel her legs were getting warmer and warmer. The fire was centimeters away from her legs. Quickly, and quietly, she muttered, "Feu proppello!" An invisible shield surrounded Teagen. The fire never reached her.

Through the flames, Teagen could see seven blurs circling the fire. She now understood why it was called the Firedance, it *did* look like they were dancing.

"Hey, boss!" one of them yelled, suddenly stopping so that the others fell on top of him like dominoes.

Zake cursed. "What the hell did you stop for, Het?" he roared.

"The girl's not burning!"

Uh oh, Teagen thought.

Zake stepped forward. "Feu naversoi," he murmured. The flames died away instantly. "You're right, Het," Zake said. "She isn't. We'll have to use another method, then, shan't we?"

56

Back at Belle's house, Lara stayed with the insane Septim while Belle ran off to get the best healer nearby. Within the hour, she returned with a nineteen-year-old female. She had long, white-blonde hair, pacific-blue eyes, moon-white skin, and a slender body; her name was Annya. Annya was a forest dweller; she, like all forest dwellers, lived in every forest that existed in Litheriä. Forest dwellers were kind, gentle people and they were the best healers you could find; however, if not treated with respect, a forest dweller could be a nasty thing to deal with.

"Insane, is he?" Annya asked Belle when she saw Septim. "I'll try my best."

Annya mumbled a few words, and jets of light-green light flew out of her fingers and wrapped themselves around Septim. The boy began to jerk violently and scream.

Lara's eyes grew wide from shock and fascination. "What's happening?" she whispered.

"This spell is causing him to go back in time up to the very moment he was perfectly sane," Annya explained.

All of a sudden, Septim froze, let out a bloodcurdling scream, and lay limp. "We should leave him be," Belle said quietly.

They filed out of the room one by one. Annya was the last one to leave. She took one look at Septim and smiled thoughtfully before closing the door.

57

When we last saw Serena, she had announced the coming of the Cursebreaker, allowing the wrong ears to hear; they were the same ears that belonged to the being that would eventually send the Cursebreaker to his doom.

Ever since then, Serena had been recruiting fighters for Cedric's army. They're creatures of all sorts: from mice to dwarves to centaurs to giants. Serena also sent chipmunk messengers to cities and forests to alert more recruits of the opportunity to fight and defeat the wicked King Hsetah.

Theo and Lorelei heard the news, and Theo was eager to join. Lorelei, on the other hand, didn't want him to. "What if something happens to you?" she argued, "What if this is a ruse of the king's to gather all his enemies and get rid of them at the same time?"

"I'll be fine, Lor," Theo argued back.

"Are you sure you'll be fine?" she cried.

"Don't you ever have faith in me?" Theo said, raising his voice. "You know I can fight well."

Lorelei looked like he had slapped her in the face. She put her hands on his shoulders. "Of course I believe in you," she said softly. "I just don't want anything to happen to you, that's all. I really do love you, Theo."

"I love you too, Lor," Theo said, "but I want to fight. I want to help."

Lorelei put her face in his shoulder and began to weep quietly. When she took a deep breath, she paused, looked at her fiancé, and said, "I just want to get married and live in peace."

"Listen, Lorelei," Theo said urgently. "If someone doesn't fight the king, nobody'll live in peace."

"But evil can never be vanquished."

"It can be. Temporarily. All we need to do is support each other, and unite to destroy our common enemy. Listen to me, I *promise* we'll get married after the war is over."

"Do you really?"

"I do."

Lorelei sighed. She knew how much this meant to him. "Oh, you win. Just come back to me in one piece, okay?"

Theo chuckled. "Okay." He then put his lips on Lorelei's and gave her a loving kiss, caressing her face tenderly. "I love you so much, Lorelei."

"I love you just as much, Theo."

58

Cedric opened his eyes. Fireball stood straight and still.

Cedric sat up. He looked at Fireball, wondering why the horse was standing rigidly. The boy followed the horse's gaze until he saw a wrapped object on the ground. He unwrapped it and a pair of glasses and note fell out into the palm of his hand. Cedric unfolded the note, which read:

These are special glasses
Used for when one trespasses
Use them as a last resort
Don't lose them or you'll go to court
Use them to leave with your lost love
Then go to the nearest and safest cove

And good luck.

The handwriting looked vaguely familiar to Cedric, but he couldn't place it. Shrugging his shoulders, the boy put the glasses and the note in his pocket. Then, after looking into the distant horizon, Cedric mounted Fireball and picked up on the trail where he had left off.

* * *

"You don't think she's dead, boss?" Leus asked hesitantly, standing over Teagen.

"No," Zake said worriedly, "but we may have pushed it too far. We'll leave her alone until we get to the castle. We should be there by sunrise tomorrow."

Teagen lay unconscious on Zenubia's back. The Surrendered Seven, realizing that the Firedance had no effect on her, whipped Teagen unconscious pitilessly. Large, red welts formed up and down her body; a small, yet visible, cut was bleeding across her cheek.

The Surrendered Seven continued riding before taking a short stop at dusk. After a small meal, they resumed their riding and continued on until daybreak, when they arrived at the foreboding gates of King Hsetah's castle.

* * *

It was two days after Cedric received the mysterious package when he finally reached the trail's end. A dark, gloomy building that held the smell of death and destruction loomed before his eyes. The black iron gates were caked with rust. Fireball shifted nervously at his side. *So, they brought her here,* Cedric thought.

Cedric knew what he must do. He led Fireball quite a distance away from the castle and tied him to a tree.

Then, taking his bow, arrows, sword, and glasses, walked back to the castle. Cedric took a deep breath, opened the creaking gates, and crossed a rickety, narrow bridge that was laid over a moat. The moat's dark waters held creatures of all sorts; all kinds of miniature sea monsters were said to dwell there. It was also said that the water itself was dangerous; if anybody fell in, the punishment was various—if you were the king's worst enemy, the water would consume you and you would disintegrate as if acid was eating you alive. If you were a friend of the king, you would just have to wait for someone to rescue you . . . before the monsters devoured you.

Cedric was relieved when he got across the bridge safely, but he didn't let his guard down. Knowing that the worst was probably yet to come, he opened the dooming, black-painted, wooden doors.

59

King Hsetah had all his guards and servants, including the Surrendered Seven, assembled before him. "When the boy comes in, allow him to enter the girl's chamber," he said, eyes scintillating with malevolence, "but make sure he does not leave, with or without her! Understood?" Everyone nodded. "Good. Leave the boy to me after that."

Everyone left to resume his or her posts.

* * *

Cedric knew something was most definitely wrong now. He met nobody since he silently entered the building. He had been expecting some sort of resistance; he doubted that the king had gone on vacation and taken everybody with him.

Cedric eventually came to a circular room that had six separate staircases leading to different places. He knew this because he saw rotting, wooden signs with peeling letters hanging above each staircase. He chose the staircase that had the sign DUNGEONS hanging over it.

Several of the large stone steps were missing, and the rest were all worn. One step was so weak, that at one point, when Cedric stepped on it, it gave way. Cedric plunged down to the deep, dark unknown below him. Only pure instinct saved him; he had grabbed onto the previous step at the last second and pulled himself up. Cedric sat on the step for a few moments to catch his breath and hopped down the rest of the stairs, testing each before trusting them with his full weight.

The steps ended, to Cedric's short-lived relief, where a long hall began. On either side of the hall were rooms that had barred doors. Cedric looked in the first few where skeletons, some of which were decapitated, lay on the floor or on tables, with dark, dry liquid splashed all over the walls and floors; some of the skeletons still had shackles on their hands or feet. Cedric felt sick. He didn't want to imagine what Teagen's captors did to her.

Finally, at the end of the hall, in the very last dungeon on a table, was where Teagen lay. Cedric tried to slide the door, but it wouldn't budge. He pulled even harder and it gave in to him. Cedric ran to the table and his eyes widened in horror as his heart was filled with several different emotions: disgust, hate, and pity; he cursed.

Teagen lay still on the table, eyes closed, wearing only two pieces of dirty madras; one was wrapped around her chest, the other around her waist. There was a long gash running from her left temple to the corner of her lower lip that was bleeding profusely. There was a vertical cut that ran from the middle of her forehead to her eyelid, crossing her eyebrow. Her legs, arms, neck, and stomach were covered in red, ugly welts. What caught Cedric's eye, though, was an odd-shaped cut surrounding Teagen's navel. It was a crudely engraved picture of a moon with an arrow going through it. *It must have been made recently,* Cedric realized, *because it's still bleeding.*

Cedric bent down and kissed Teagen's hot forehead and held her hand. "You poor thing," he murmured.

"Poor thing indeed," said a low, mocking voice from behind.

60

Cedric slowly turned around. A frightening figure in a black cloak and hood stood before him, with the door lying on the floor. "Who-who're you?" Cedric stammered.

This response was a shock to King Hsetah. Everyone knew who he was; that's what he thought until now. "I am the king," he hissed. "Who else do you think I am?"

Suddenly, the boy's surprised voice turned cold. "Did you do this to Teagen?" Cedric asked, voice shaking with suppressed rage.

"Well," came the answer, "yes. And no."

"What do you mean?" Cedric asked suspiciously.

"What do you mean?" the king mimicked in a high voice. Then, he cackled. "*What do I mean?* I mean that I gave the order to have her abducted—and tortured, along the way—and brought here."

Cedric's blood began to boil. "For what reason?"

"*Oh*, the little itty-bitty Cursebreaker doesn't know?" King Hsetah taunted. "To bring you here, of course."

Cedric felt a chill run up and down spine. His mouth unexpectedly became dry. "Why?" he croaked.

"To kill you," hissed the king. "I knew you'd come after the girl, and I was right."

"B-but *why?*"

"Unbelievable," King Hsetah, completely surprised. "I now pity all those people who count on you. Ha! '*Why?*' Are you *really* that thick? Haven't you read the prophecies, boy?" The king began to circle Cedric and Teagen in the room, his cloak swishing at his heels. "They talked about the Cursebreaker destroying me. I'm not going to stand like a lollipop and not do anything. And that is why I'm going to kill you." King Hsetah was standing in front of the doorway again. "Now."

The king pulled a spear from the air. It was pure metal down to the very bottom of the stick, which held the polished point. Cedric was horrified. He didn't want to die. At least, not now. Then, something crossed his mind: "*. . . Use them as a last resort . . . Use them to leave with your last love. . . .*" The glasses! He considered this the time to wear them. But first, he instinctively unsheathed his sword.

The king threw his head back and laughed. "A sword!" he cried, tears of mirth coming down his face. "A mere *sword!* Pathetic! You'll have to do better than that next time! Oops! I forgot . . . *There won't be a next time!*"

Then, King Hsetah threw the spear at Cedric. The boy held up his sword as he would a shield. When the spear point connected with the sword blade, the spear itself shattered into a million pieces and disappeared

The king was stunned. "That—That's the Sword of Damaé," he said quietly.

While he was talking, Cedric fumbled with the glasses as he sheathed his weapon. A miraculous event occurred when Cedric put the glasses on; he turned invisible. "... *Use them to leave with your lost love* ..."

Cedric knew what he must do. He held Teagen in his arms; she turned invisible, too. Since the door had been taken out of its frame, Cedric stepped around the king—who was waving his arms wildly, trying to find his invisible prisoners—and into the hallway. Cedric took off at a run; he left the way he had come only half an hour before. Nobody saw him. When he finally left the ugly gates, he ran all the way back to Fireball.

"... *Then go to the nearest and safest cove* ..." He had to go to the nearest and safest cove. Cedric mounted Fireball, with Teagen resting against him, took the glasses off, and kicked Fireball's sides to get the horse to gallop as fast as possible.

* * *

Back at the castle, the king howled as he gripped his hood in anger and frustration. "THEY GOT AWAY!" he roared. "And the fool boy has my sword, too! That—little—THIEF!" King Hsetah lowered his head in dismay and cursed Cedric with the most sinister expletives he knew. "This means *war*," he growled.

* * *

Cedric found a small cove far away from the castle. However, to his shock and sorrow, he found Zenubia there, too. She lay on her side and was bleeding from opened wounds in the side of her neck and her stomach. It was a grisly sight. After putting Teagen down on the ground, he rushed over to the feeble horse; there was no point. He knew it was too late. "Zenubia," he whispered, "you were, and still are, a terrific horse. We'll never forget you." Cedric rubbed the horse's ears as he said this. He smiled through silent tears when Zenubia let out a small snort. Cedric bowed his head and quietly cried when the horse exhaled its last breath. After a moment's silence, Cedric went back to where Teagen was.

"Oh, Cedric," she whispered after she regained consciousness.

Cedric dropped down by her side, "You're alive!" he whispered with contentment.

Teagen smiled. Or tried to. "I love you, Cedric."

"I love you, too, Teagen."

"Do me a favor."

"Anything."

Teagen took a shuddering, deep breath after a small wave of pain washed over her. "Say 'naversoi' and . . . think of . . . Belle's house. And hold my hand . . . and . . . Fireball's rein's, as well . . ."

Teagen slipped back into unconsciousness as Cedric did what she told him to do. In a whirlwind, they vanished from the cove and appeared in Belle's sitting room.

61

There was a scream. "Teagen!" Lara rushed forward as Cedric settled Teagen down on the sofa. "Cedric, what happened?"

Cedric told Lara and Belle everything that had happened since he left after Belle had put Fireball outside. When he finished, Belle stood up and said, "I'm getting Annya."

She went into another room and came back with the healer. Introductions were quickly made, and Annya took a look at Teagen's wounds. "Bring her to the room," she ordered Cedric.

He picked Teagen up and laid her down on the bed he had slept in just a week ago as Septim was waking up. "Hiya, Cedric!" Septim said cheerfully. Then he saw Teagen. "What happened?"

"I need you both out," Annya said.

"Well, well, well," Septim said, winking at Cedric, "Who might this be?"

"OUT!"

The two walked out of the room in silence. Cedric recounted everything that had happened. "Blimey," Septim said, speechless.

"How've you been?" Cedric asked, trying to change the subject.

"Very well. That healer is absolutely beautiful, isn't she?"

Cedric shrugged. "She's all yours."

"Think I should court her?"

"Go ahead."

"When she comes out o' the room, I'll ask her."

"Cedric?" Belle said, coming up to him.

Cedric turned to her. "Yes?"

"I've heard rumors that your army is preparing."

Cedric stiffened and then relaxed. "Are you up to fighting?" Belle inquired softly.

"Course I am," came the curt reply. "After what the king and his henchmen did to Teagen and Zenubia, I'm ready to tear them apart with my own bare hands."

"We'll need that kind of leader who has a solid reason to fight, you know."

"Don't worry. I'm never going to rest until the king is dead."

"You could die, you know that, don't you?" Belle said in an almost inaudible voice.

"Of course I know that!"

"So, are you ready to fight?"

Cedric's eyes glinted with determination and his face was set with a resolved expression. "I am."

COMING SOON!

The second Installment In
The Cursebreaker Trilogy . . .

The Cursebreaker II: The Battle